DAW

P9-EDJ-387

Critics Rave About Simon Brett and His Charles Paris Mysteries:

"Paris is probably current crime fiction's most complex and developed series character and . . . Simon Brett is the best serial mystery writer now setting pen to paper."

—*Sun-Times* (Chicago)

"Brett knows the British stage inside out, and his backgrounds are unusually authentic."

—Newgate Callendar,
The New York Times Book Review

"Quite simply the best in the business!"

—*Kirkus Reviews*

"Simon Brett, the Laurence Olivier of the theatrical mystery, writes thrillers that play wonderfully: the dialogue is witty and natural, the characterization engagingly complex, and the plots most cunningly constructed."

—*Booklist*

"Solid entertainment. . . . Brett's insider's knowledge of show business . . . makes his witty mysteries go!"

—*Time*

OTHER DELL MYSTERIES BY SIMON BRETT:

Situation Tragedy
Murder Unprompted
Murder in the Title

COMING SOON FROM DELL:

Cast, in Order of Disappearance
So Much Blood
Star Trap
An Amateur Corpse
A Comedian Dies
The Dead Side of the Mike

Not Dead, Only Resting

Simon Brett

A DELL BOOK

Published by
Dell Publishing Co., Inc.
1 Dag Hammarskjold Plaza
New York, New York 10017

Dell ® TM 681510, Dell Publishing Co., Inc.

ISBN: 0-440-16442-7

Reprinted by arrangement with Charles Scribner's Sons

Printed in the United States of America
First Dell printing—January 1986

To Chris

"With respect to the extravagance of actors, as a traditional character, it is not to be wondered at. They live from hand to mouth: they plunge from want into luxury; they have no means of making money *breed*, and all professions that do not live by turning money into money, or have not a certainty of accumulating it in the end by parsimony, spend it. Uncertain of the future, they make sure of the present moment. This is not unwise."

WILLIAM HAZLITT (1778–1830)
"On Actors and Acting"

Chapter One

TRYST WAS NOT Charles Paris's usual scene. It was an expensive restaurant, very fashionable with the most successful members—and, in many cases, the gayest members—of the theatrical profession. Charles Paris was an indigent actor on whom success had rarely smiled, and he was unarguably heterosexual.

But that Saturday evening at the end of August he was the guest of two men who were ideally qualified as clients of Tryst. William Bartlemas and Kevin O'Rourke formed mutually a phenomenon of the British theatre. Though both had, way back in prehistory, been actors, they had long since given up performing in favour of a spreading collection of theatrical memorabilia connected with two great actors, Edmund Kean and William Macready. Fuelled by Bartlemas's substantial private income, they scoured the country for relics of their idols, returning religiously to London for the opening of every show at a West End theatre, where their first night presence in the fifth row of the stalls was regarded by managements with the awe that soothsayers reserve for comets. The couple's habits of dressing identically and talking in an unending shared monologue were just the kind of eccentricities to endear them to the British theatrical establishment, and possibly no one "in the business" enjoyed greater universal goodwill. Certainly, when a chance meeting the previous week had led to his invitation, Charles Paris had leapt at the opportunity of spending an evening in Bartlemas and O'Rourke's company.

"It's lovely to see them making such a *go* of it . . ." William Bartlemas was commenting on the success of Tryst.

"Really humming with the right sort of people . . ." Kevin O'Rourke concurred.

"Sir John over there . . ."

"Maggie with someone new . . ."

"And he's so young. I swear that's how she keeps her complexion—melts down young actors for their glands . . ."

"Hmm. Ooh, and look who Bernard Walton's with . . ."

"Well, there's a turn-up. And what does her husband say, I wonder . . . ?"

"*Super* fodder for the gossip columns . . ."

"*Super*. Oh, look, there's Bertram Pride doing his 'I am a celebrity' number . . ."

"Well, after that *Lexton and Sons* series, he is . . . almost . . ."

"Who's the pretty girl he's with . . . ?"

"Don't know. A late booking from Rent-A-Tottie, perhaps . . . ?"

O'Rourke's sally brought a shriek of laughter from Bartlemas. It ended with a breath-pause, when Charles almost had a chance to say something, but O'Rourke beat him to it. "Oh yes, dear, *but all* the right people here . . ."

"Including . . ." Bartlemas inclined his head towards Charles. "Including of course our guest . . ."

Charles Paris grinned wryly. "Not in the same league as that lot, I'm afraid."

"Now come on, don't do yourself down . . ."

"He's so modest, isn't he, Bartlemas . . . ?"

"Far too modest. Always has been . . ."

"You're a very fine actor, always have been . . ."

"Never forget your Bassanio, will we . . . ?"

"Lovely Bassanio . . ."

"Anyway, tell me, Charles . . ." Bartlemas put on an expression of mock-seriousness. "What's next for you?"

"What's next?" asked Charles, puzzled.

"Yes, dear. Work. What are you doing at the moment?"

"Ah." Charles grinned again, this time ruefully. "At the moment I am 'resting'."

"Oh dear . . ."

"Oh well, sure something'll turn up soon . . ."

"Been resting long, have you?"

"Except for two days on a radio play last week, it's just coming up for three months."

"Oh."

"I am rested to the point of torpor."

"Bad luck, Charles. Still, it's happened before."

"Many times."

"You've had your little patches out of work since you started."

"It might be more accurate to say, Bartlemas, that I've had my little patches *in* work."

"Well . . . Something'll turn up."

"Oh yes," Charles agreed. "Micawberism is the only philosophy for an actor."

"Who's your agent?" asked O'Rourke. "Does he beaver away on your behalf . . . ?"

"Maurice Skellern," Charles replied.

The faces of the other two fell.

"Oh . . ."

"Oh dear . . ."

"Hardly a human dynamo, is he?"

"No," said Charles.

"And what about that lovely wife of yours . . . ?"

"Dear Frances . . ."

"You two back together again, are you . . . ?"

"I'm afraid not. Frances is having a wild affair with a schools inspector . . ."

"Oh dear . . ."

"That sounds serious . . ."

"I'm afraid it is. When I last spoke to her she was asking about our getting a divorce."

"What, to marry this . . . ?"

Charles nodded, suddenly too emotional for speech. His hosts could not pretend they hadn't noticed the change of mood, and there was an uneasy silence, ended by the timely arrival at their table of Tristram Gowers, who owned the restaurant and whose name had provided its punning title.

"Bartlemas, O'Rourke—*my dears*!"

The flamboyance of his greeting betrayed his background as a professional actor. Indeed, like many actors who go into other professions, Tristram Gowers seemed at times as if he was playing the part of a restaurateur rather than actually *being* one. He dressed invariably in a black velvet suit, with a froth of green silk scarf at his neck. He was a little under six foot, and carried himself as if holding in an unruly stomach. His hands flashed with rings, which, in spite of their value, looked as if they had just been collected from the props cupboard; and his face, too, seemed to have been dressed for the part of an Identikit restaurateur in a revue sketch. Over-large glasses with transparent rims gave him an owlish appearance. His walrus moustache was obviously real, but contrived to look as if it owed its adherence to spirit gum. The silver-grey toupé which crowned his characterization made no pretence at reality. Though it lacked an actual pigtail, it had the air of something devised by Wig Creations for a Restoration drama.

In fact, Charles noted around him three contrasting examples of hairdressing artifice. The wiry remnants of Bartlemas's hair were brushed up into a foam of dyed ginger; O'Rourke's surviving strands were trained across his scalp like piped icing over a birthday cake; but for sheer audacity Tristram Gowers' toupé collected all available awards. Whereas the others still tried to maintain the illusion of natural growth, Tristram had found baldness the stimulus to the creation of a new art form.

The restaurateur clasped Kevin O'Rourke's small face between his large hands. "O coz, coz, coz, my pretty little coz, how are you?"

Charles would have put down the quotation from *As You Like It* to mere theatrical flamboyance, had not Bartlemas whispered, "True, you know, they are cousins . . ."

"Really?"

"Oh yes," Tristram Gowers and Kevin O'Rourke asserted together.

"Have you met Charles Paris, Trist . . . ?" asked Bartlemas.

The brown eyes behind the owl glasses took Charles in for a moment before saying, "No, I don't think so. Of course, I know the name."

If that was the way he wanted to play it, Charles didn't mind. He could understand why Tristram Gowers might be embarrassed about their previous meeting. True, it had been some fifteen years before and the amnesia might be genuine. But Charles suspected that Tristram did not wish to be reminded of the time before he "came out", the time when he had still been married to the actress, Zoë Fratton, before he met Yves Lafeu and discovered his real nature.

It was as if Charles's thought of Yves prompted Bartlemas's next question. "And how is Him In The Kitchen, Trist . . . ?"

"Very nice," Tristram Gowers replied, with a coy smile.

"Being a good boy or a naughty boy . . . ?"

Charles recognized this as a reference to Yves Lafeu's occasional promiscuity. Though the restaurateur and his chef were very much a couple, the younger man enjoyed sporadic infidelities. These led to blazing rows between the two, rows which often erupted openly in the restaurant, and which, indeed, were regarded by regulars as one of the attractions of Tryst.

"Goodish," Tristram replied judiciously. "Occasional lapses. Picked up a nasty little trollop down at the Sparta couple of weeks back."

Bartlemas and O'Rourke giggled at this reference. Charles assumed the Sparta must be some sort of gay club.

"Had to put a stop to that very quickly," Tristram continued in a schoolmistressy way. "Still, all be fine now. For a whole month I'm not going to let him out of my sight."

"What do you mean?"

"Hols, Bartlemas, hols. *Fermeture annuelle*."

"Oh?"

"Didn't you know, dear? Didn't you read the notice on the door?"

"No."

"We close down for September every year. Go away for the whole month. We've got this house near Cahors. Didn't you *know*? Oh, I tell you, dears, you're very lucky to get seats tonight of all nights. As of tomorrow, poor London has a whole month of being Tryst-less."

"*Quelle tristesse*," sighed O'Rourke, and was rewarded by gales of giggles.

"So when are you actually off?" asked Bartlemas, as the hysteria subsided.

"Soon as we've tidied up here," Tristram Gowers replied. "What we do every year. Get the restaurant in order, lock up and away we go. Six-thirty ferry from Dover tomorrow morning, then we just drive on from Calais till we get to Mas-de-Pouzard."

"Which is where you have the house?"

"Uhuh. Eleven kilometres outside Cahors. Wonderful views over the River Lot. Pure heaven."

"Don't you stop on the way down?"

"No, love, we just press on till we're there. Share the driving. We can't relax until we're actually *there*."

"You don't even stop for the odd *menu gastronomique* . . . ?"

"No, we're positively monastic in our restraint. I sort out sandwiches which we eat on the way. Mind you, once we're *there*, then we *really* start serious eating." Tristram smiled in delicious anticipation.

"Does Yves come from that part of France?" asked Bartlemas.

"No, dear. My 'in-laws'—whom I have yet to have the pleasure of meeting—and may that pleasure be eternally deferred—live in Reims. Very solid, I gather. *Petit bourgeois*—with the emphasis on the 'petty'."

"So," asked Charles, "you close up here, then pack and—?"

"No, dear, no. The whole operation has been organized for *weeks*. Everything's packed already. The Volvo's stuffed to the gills. I've done it all, of course. Yves, the 'great chef', is far too *sensitive* to deal with the minutiae of life." The mockery of the emphasis was not wholly friendly. "Still, I suppose it makes sense. Though I say it myself, I can state, without unbecoming immodesty, that I am one of the world's great packers. I begin by emptying the car completely, get it as clean as an operating theatre, and then start the actual packing. It is a work of art when I've finished, you know. I know exactly where everything is. Which is just as well, because I don't get much help from *him* when it comes to unpacking."

"So what time do you have to leave?"

"Try and get away by half-past three. Should be no problem. The flat's all tidied up; passports, currency, tickets . . . all sorted out."

Tristram Gowers' obsessive pride in his organizational skills was beginning to grate on Charles, so he was quite relieved when the restaurateur changed the subject and, prefacing his question with a huge "*Anyway*", asked, "what are you going to eat tonight?"

"Is Yves . . ." asked Bartlemas breathlessly, "doing his *divine* . . ."

"But *divine* . . ."

"Sucking pig?"

Tristram held the pause dramatically, then announced, "He is."

"Three sucking pigs, please, Trist . . ."

While they ate their *pâté en croute*, Bartlemas and O'Rourke regaled Charles with lavish descriptions of the main course, and when it arrived the sucking pig lived up to their Roget's *Thesaurus* of superlatives. Perhaps because of their conversation with Tristram, they drank the strong black wine of Cahors, and Charles began to feel better.

The ache of his feelings for Frances and the nag of being out of work both dulled. He felt whole, eating and drinking well, with entertaining friends, in pleasant surroundings.

The decor of Tryst was dark red, and the walls were liberally scattered with gilt-framed playbills and old tinted prints of actors long-dead.

"They have got some lovely stuff . . ." Bartlemas observed, as he mopped up the last juices of sucking pig with bread.

"Divine memorabilia . . ."

"Nothing to do with Edmund Kean of course . . ."

"Or William Macready . . ."

"Of course . . ."

"I mean, they wouldn't *dare* . . ."

"Tristram knows we'd scratch his eyes out if he dared buy anything and not offer it to us . . ."

"Yes. Actually, you know," said O'Rourke airily, "Tristram's going to leave all his theatrical stuff to me . . ."

"Ooh, you big fibber!"

"It's true, Bartlemas, true. Scout's honour. He said if he and Yves both died in a car accident or something, then I could have it . . ."

"Oh yes?"

"Yes. I am his cousin, you know . . ."

"Of course . . ."

"Nearest relative . . ."

"Hmm . . ."

Charles looked round the restaurant, as Bartlemas and O'Rourke went through the motions of some formal private squabble. It was strange to see the rich end of the acting profession. As with people in most businesses, Charles tended to mix with actors of about the same eminence and income as himself, but in the theatre the identity of those people changed more quickly than in other areas. Most actors had in them the potential for sudden failure or prosperity. A coincidence, a sudden break, could lift any one of them to stardom; overexposure, one part badly played, or just the lack of suitable jobs, could bring any one of them quickly down to the semi-anonymity of most of their profession.

Charles could see examples of the system at work in that room. Bernard Walton. They'd worked together at the beginning of the younger man's career, and Charles had acted as a kind of mentor to Bernard. But then television sit-coms and the West End had turned Bernard into a household name, earning considerably more in the average month than Charles did in a good year. Charles felt glad that he had his back to the star and could only see a reflection in the glass of one of the playbills. He didn't want to be recognized and drowned in Bernard Walton's patronizing bonhomie.

Bertram Pride—there was another example. He had been a perfectly competent actor in his early thirties, going round the reps dutifully, giving his juve leads in bedroom farces, second leads in Shakespeares—Laertes in *Hamlet*, Sebastian in *Twelfth Night*, Macduff in *Macbeth*, that sort of thing—unbending a little as one of the Ugly Sisters in a pantomime—and then suddenly a lucky break had found him cast as Philip Lexton in the television series *Lexton and Sons*. This had been one of those unpromising family business sagas, which had turned out to be addictive viewing. The first series had built its audience steadily enough to be followed by a second, then a third, a fourth, a fifth. Gossip said that the sequence had now finally come to an end, but it had done enough to raise Bertram Pride to a kind of stardom.

He had got the money from the original programmes, fees rising as the series' popularity increased. Then the money for the domestic repeats and the foreign sales. On a big success, that could multiply the basic fees by many hundred per cent.

Added to the direct financial benefit from the series, there were the spin-offs. As a well-known television face, he would be invited on to other television shows. He would submit to panel games, unroll anecdotes on chat-shows, be offered feature roles in one-off plays. His face and voice would become disproportionately valuable to advertising companies. He would be paid handsomely for personal appearances to open supermarkets, to host sales conferences. He would, in short, have become a personality. And even though the series that launched him had ended, he had surely by now achieved sufficient momentum to keep him going for the rest of his career.

And all that from one lucky break, Charles thought ruefully. He looked across to where Bertram Pride, conscious that people in the restaurant recognized him, joked with his Rent-A-Tottie. Perhaps the movement of Charles's head caught the "star"'s eye, because he suddenly focused on their table and gave a wave of recognition to Bartlemas and O'Rourke. Then, seeming to decide that this acknowledgement was insufficient, he clasped his Rent-A-Tottie by the hand and came across to greet them.

"Bartlemas . . . O'Rourke . . ."

"Bertram . . ."

The effusiveness of the greeting was automatic.

"Have you met Charles Paris?"

"Don't think so. Know the name, *of course.*"

Charles was getting used to that response. It's always a safe reaction when one is introduced to an unknown actor, since it discreetly veils ignorance in the implication that one has followed his career from the very beginnings with unflagging interest.

Bertram waved airily at his Rent-A-Tottie. "And this is Henry."

The girl smiled with a little adolescent jerk of her head, and Charles saw how very young she was. Pretty, though. Almost white blond hair that curled in little tendrils at her temples. Blue eyes so widely innocent as to be nearly embarrassing, and skin glowing as softly as if it had just been rubbed with baby powder. Her neat little figure was emphasized by the expensive simplicity of a white pleated cotton dress with lacy collar and cuffs.

"Henry, these are Bartlemas and O'Rourke, who I'm sure you've heard of."

"Absolutely," she enthused, immediately placing herself in that area of the upper classes where "absolutely" is used to mean "yes".

"What are you up to at the moment, Bertram . . . ?"

"Yes, what are you *doing* . . . ?"

"Oh, not a lot. Few things in the air."

Charles supposed *he* could have answered the question with the same airy nonchalance, but somehow didn't think he'd carry it off. He couldn't have infused the words with the same implications of producers falling over themselves to employ him.

"One interesting thing . . . change of direction . . ." Bertram went on. "Actually got a book coming out next month."

"Really? What, are you turning into a Frederick Forsyth . . . ?"

"Or a Harold Robbins . . . ?"

"Oh God, no. Not fiction. Autobiographical thing, actually. Amazed to be asked. Showman Books are bringing it out."

"Have you written it yourself?"

"Oh, pretty well, yes. Well, I nattered into a tape recorder for a few days, and then some chap sort of breaks it into chapters and puts in the full stops. Being serialized in the *Sunday Express*, actually."

"Oh?"

"As I say, I was amazed to be asked, but this chap at Showman Books seems convinced there's a market. *Lexton and Sons* did get such an enormous following."

"Yes. Is the rumour true . . . ?"

"That there aren't going to be any more . . . ?"

"Oh yes, I think we really have run that into the ground. All want to go off and do our own things now. You know, very grateful for the success and all that, but can't stand still in this business."

There were murmurs of agreement. The girl, Henry, looked awkward and a little lost. "Are you in the business too?" Charles asked.

"Well, yes." She blushed. "I mean, sort of. Just out of drama school. Starting out, you know."

"I see."

"Frightfully difficult, making a start, you know. You have to get this Equity card. If you haven't got that, it's hopeless."

Charles was amused at her explaining his profession to him, but didn't comment.

"Never mind, dear," said Bartlemas. "I'm sure Bertram can give you a helping hand . . ."

"The odd tip . . ." O'Rourke agreed.

"Oh yes, I'll teach her a thing or two. We're going down to my cottage in Kent for the weekend."

Bertram Pride's abrupt change to undoubted sexual innuendo brought a new blush to Henry's face and an awkward stop to the conversation. It was fortunate that the arrival of the couple's sweet course provided a reason for moving.

"Better get back to our profiteroles," said Bertram.

Charles watched the "star" back to his table. Bertram was tall and his brown hair was cropped very short. (Charles wondered idly if that meant he had just been working on another period serial. Television's love-affair with the first three decades of the twentieth century had led to a lot of actors walking around with short-back-and-sides.)

Strange, how someone like Bertram, who had only been thought moderately good-looking before his success, was now, thanks to the mythologizing power of television, accepted as an archetype of masculine beauty. And presumably would have no problem in picking up any number of delicious little Henries.

And what of Bertram Pride's talent? Good, yes. As good as a few thousand other actors who could have done as well, given the same opportunities. Yet again, Charles was struck by the strange values that obtained in his profession.

He did not feel jealous. He had long since accepted the lottery nature of acting.

He wouldn't have minded a bit of Bertram Pride's income, though.

Bartlemas's voice brought him back from his musing. "No, the one over there on the door. I'm sure it is . . ."

"The one behind the bar. She looks much more like Yves . . ."

Charles's quizzical look brought an explanation from O'Rourke. "Yves's sister. Apparently Yves's sister has started working here. Name of Monique. We were trying to sort out which one she was . . ."

"I'd *put money* on the one by the door," asserted Bartlemas.

"Really. I mean, she's got that pout . . . just like Yves when he's throwing a moody. So tall, though. He's got all the looks . . ."

"Yes, but really, dear, the colouring. It must be the one behind the bar. Just like Yves. And she's so petite . . ."

"Go on, Charles love, you must decide . . ."

"*Arbitrate*, that's the word . . ."

"Yes, *arbitrate* for us . . ."

Charles shrugged. "I'm sorry. I'd love to, but I'm afraid I've never met Yves, so I can't be much help."

"Never met Yves!" Bartlemas threw his hands to his mouth in mock-amazement. "But I thought you were bound to have worked together when he was a choreographer . . ."

"Two left feet, I'm afraid," said Charles. "Never had a lot to do with shows that had choreographers."

"Oh, but you—"

"Never mind." O'Rourke stilled his partner with a gesture. "Charles will have the opportunity to meet Yves *now*."

The other two followed his outstretched hand towards the figure who issued from the kitchen.

Yves Lafeu was beautiful, and knew it. His colouring was not typically French; the translucent blue eyes and flopping blond hair made him look more Teutonic than anything; only the olivey sheen of his skin, heightened by sweat from the kitchen, gave him a Latin air. He was dressed in the traditional white jacket and checked trousers of a French chef, though a spotted handkerchief knotted round his neck turned the image into something insolent and piratical.

The grace with which he moved showed his dancer's training. His step had a self-mocking tartiness as he moved across the restaurant, waving in acknowledgement of his guests, most of whom applauded his entrance. It was obviously a Tryst ritual for him to appear at the end of the evening's cooking to receive his due of praise.

He came first to Bartlemas and O'Rourke's table, clutching one of their hands in each of his with genuine affection. "My dears!" His heavy French accent contained the same element of self-parody as his walk. "Trist said you were in tonight, and I'm just so . . . *enchanté* to see you both."

"You're looking younger than ever . . ." said Bartlemas.

"And more beautiful . . ." agreed O'Rourke.

Yves made a self-depreciating moue. "All bridgework and vanishing cream, *mes chéris*."

"But now you're here, you can settle a dispute for us . . ."

"Yes, you can . . ."

"But I did not think you two had *disputations*. I thought you were the perfect couple. I thought it was only Trist and me who—"

"No, not a dispute, just a disagreement . . ."

"That's all . . ."

"We just want to know which of these pretty young ladies . . ."

"Is your sister."

"Ah, Monique." Yves nodded lugubriously. "*Ma petite soeur*. Well, she is—"

He turned towards the entrance, confirming Bartlemas's speculation. The tall girl by the door, with the long dark hair, was Monique Lafeu. Around thirty, with a discontented expression.

But what her brother saw when he turned to her stopped him dead.

Monique's job was to check the reservations and take the coats of the arriving guests. When they looked at her, she was doing this service for a tall young man with unnaturally blond hair. He wore a blue and white striped shirt and tight beige trousers. A matching jacket was slung over-casually across his shoulders. He appeared to be questioning something about the reservation.

Yves moved across the room, mesmerized by the young man's appearance. "Gary," he murmured, opening his arms to welcome him.

The newcomer looked up. The expression on his face was at first one of total surprise; then recognition and pleasure took over. "Yves."

But before the two met, a voice from the kitchen entrance stopped them in their tracks. "Get out!"

Everyone in the restaurant turned to look at Tristram Gowers. His face beneath the toupé was bright red. In his hand he carried a large Sabatier kitchen knife.

He moved across the room towards the two young men, who still stood frozen. "Get out, you little tart," he hissed at the boy called Gary.

21

"But why? I've got a date here." The young man's defiance was not very convincing. His manner of speech was stagey and elocuted, like a chorus boy from a musical given his first speaking part.

"How dare you—"

"No, I have, I have. My name's Gary Stane and I'm meant to be meeting a Mr Carruthers. For dinner. It was arranged."

"Get out!" Tristram Gowers gestured with the knife.

"I don't see why I should. I have a perfect right to—"

But the next, closer, gesture of the knife stopped his expostulation. Deciding discretion to be the better part of valour, the boy called Gary turned on his heel and slipped out of the restaurant.

Tristram turned to his lover. "How you dare . . . how you have the nerve to invite your nasty, dirty little bit of Sparta rough trade into my restaurant—"

"But I did not. I was not expecting him. He just came. It was not—"

"Get into the kitchen!" Tristram shouted.

Yves pouted his lips as if to reply, but then thought better of it and, with an exaggerated swing of his hips, minced off to the kitchen.

Tristram Gowers moved across to the bar and poured himself a heavy slug of Armagnac from a bottle pivoted in a wrought-iron container. He downed it in one, then let the kitchen knife fall on to the the bar in the silent restaurant.

This was the cue for conversation at the tables to restart. The cabaret was over.

"Someone," said William Bartlemas, in the voice of a long-suffering children's nanny, "could do with a holiday."

Chapter Two

CHARLES'S APPOINTMENT TO sign on at the Unemployment Office that Monday was not until half-past eleven. He always tried to fix the visit so that he could go straight to a lunchtime drink. He could usually guarantee to meet another acting acquaintance in the queue, and rather jolly sessions in the pub often ensued. Charles got to know that pub well. His visits to the office were more regular than those of most unemployed. Once they'd signed on, they'd receive their Giro cheques in the post. Because Charles lived in a house divided into bedsitters, his was reckoned to be an "unsafe address", so he had to go and collect in person.

The trendiest Unemployment Office for actors is the one in Chadwick Street near Westminster Abbey, but Charles went to the one in Lisson Grove, which was a brisk half-hour walk from his Hereford Road bedsitter. Though it has not got quite the cachet of Chadwick Street, the staff there do at least know about actors, who aren't subjected to the endless questioning about their lack of work which they sometimes experience in provincial offices.

Almost all Equity members have had to sign on at some point or other; it's part of the job. Even so-called "household names" will get back on the register immediately they finish their current job. In fact, stage-struck autograph-hunters would do much better hanging round the entrances at Chadwick Street and Lisson Grove than they would at the stage doors of West End theatres.

But, though he didn't expect any more than a cursory questioning about his job prospects—if even that—Charles decided he'd show willing and ring his agent. He had an hour to kill before he set off for Lisson Grove and . . . well, you never knew—something might have come up.

It hadn't.

"No," said Maurice Skellern's voice predictably. "It really isn't a very good time at the moment."

"Is it ever?"

"Well, no, Charles, not really. I mean, all the television companies are cutting back on production, the provincial reps have mostly settled their companies for the autumn season—"

"When we last spoke, you said they hadn't yet started to select their companies for the autumn season."

"No. Well, they must have done it in the interim since we spoke, Charles. I haven't heard of any auditions coming up, and you know how close I keep my ear to the ground, don't you?"

Yes, about as close as an orbiting space satellite, thought Charles. But he didn't say it.

"I did hear of one open audition coming up, actually."

"Oh."

"For a musical, though . . ."

"Oh. Well . . ."

"Never been your strong suit, musicals, have they, Charles?"

"I wouldn't say that." (OLD ACTORS' RULE: Never admit you can't do anything. If the part requires tap-dancing or horse-riding or scuba-diving or deaf-and-dumb language, of course you can do it. Let the truth come out once rehearsals have started and the contract has been signed. Much of an actor's life he spends following the principle enunciated in the old joke:

"Are you Jewish?"

"Not necessarily."

An actor is not *necessarily* anything; but when the occasion arises, he can be *everything*.)

"Trouble is, Charles, this musical's all kids. No part for anyone over sixteen."

"Oh." Charles offered no further opposition. Though actors should think themselves capable of everything, there are moments when it is prudent for them to recognize their limitations.

"Nothing doing on the commercial scene, I suppose, Maurice?"

"Not a lot. Bit iffy, that, at the moment. There's this dispute brewing between Equity and Channel Four over rates for commercials, and a lot of the production companies are holding fire until that's resolved. Presumably it'll be sorted out once Channel Four actually starts in November, but . . ."

"Yes . . ."

"Otherwise, doesn't look too wonderful . . ."

"No . . ."

"I don't suppose you heard of anything coming up when you did that radio last week . . ."

"No . . ."

"No . . ." The conversation was becoming becalmed in unfinished sentences.

"Ooh, one thing," said Maurice suddenly.

"Yes?" Charles was instantly alert.

"Did I tell you I was off on holiday next week?"

"No. Somewhere nice?"

"Oh, just the Canaries."

Just the Canaries. It was dismissed as if it had been Littlehampton. Charles tried to remember when he had last had a holiday. How did Maurice manage it? Certainly not on ten per cent of Charles Paris's earnings. Not even on fifteen per cent, thought Charles, remembering ruefully that his agent had recently raised his commission rate. So where did Maurice get his money from? He mentioned occasional other clients, but none of them were much more successful than Charles. Perhaps Maurice had one huge international star on his books, whose earnings subsidized all the rest . . . ? It seemed unlikely that that could be kept a secret. Nor would it be in Maurice's nature to want to keep it a secret. No, he must have some other source of income. Inherited wealth seemed improbable, so what was it? A string of launderettes? A hamburger franchise? White slave traffic? Charles somehow knew he would never find out the real answer.

He also felt a kind of emptiness at the prospect of Maurice being away. His agent never *did* ring with amazing offers of work, but the fantasy that he *might* remained intact; when he was away, even that possibility was gone.

"How long are you away?"

"Just the fortnight."

Again the casual "just".

"Well, have a good time."

"I'll try to. Could certainly do with a break."

From what? Charles restrained himself from asking the question.

"Fine. Yes, well, Maurice, if anything does come up in the next few days, be sure and let me know."

"Charles, you know me."

Yes, I do. That's why I said "be sure and let me know".

"Ooh, one thing."

Again the words commanded Charles's full attention. "Yes?"

"Do you know a Casting Director at West End Television called Dana Wilson?"

"No."

"Oh well, I might be meeting her socially tomorrow. I'll put in a word."

"Thanks."

"Maybe set up a general interview for you."

"That'd be nice."

"Yes. Not that they're casting anything at the moment, though."

As he always did when he put the phone down after talking to Maurice Skellern, Charles wondered whether he ought to change his agent. It's a common feeling among unemployed actors, their special version of the unsuccessful workman blaming his tools. Some greet every bout of "resting" as an invitation to start ringing round other agents to set up interviews.

But they all come up against the same Catch-22. They go in to see the new agent, explaining that they're currently out of work, reeling off lists of credits, possibly showing portfolios of press cuttings and photographs, and saying that their current agent just doesn't seem to be trying to get anything for them. The new agent is very nice, very sympathetic, says yes it does seem amazing that someone with credits like that isn't working, and yes he hasn't heard very good reports of the other agent, and certainly he might consider taking the actor on. At this point the actor beams. Then the agent says that of course he couldn't commit himself finally until he's seen the potential client work. Is there a chance of seeing something he's in? Well, no, there isn't, that's the whole point, he's out of work. Oh dear. But there was that television series earlier in the year, I had a good part in that, says the actor. Kicking himself for the omission, the agent regrets that somehow he failed to see a single episode. (At this point, a clued-up actor may try to call the agent's bluff by producing a video cassette of the show. Only momentarily fazed, the agent will be very grateful for the idea, but regret that the office video is on the blink, or that he's only got one at home and he wouldn't want to run the risk of losing such a precious record, so he doesn't feel it would be fair on the potential client for him to take it.) Then, apologetic that he really must get on with some work, the agent ushers his visitor out of the office, suggesting that maybe the actor and some friends should get together a lunchtime fringe show. He'd love to come and see that. End of interview.

(The few who do actually make the effort to put on a fringe show encounter a new twist to the storyline. They write to or ring up the apparently interested agent well in advance of the performances and receive copious assurances that he will move heaven and earth to witness the actor working. Other agents, notified of the show, are equally grateful for the golden opportunity they are being offered. The week of performance comes, and the cast play their hearts out every lunchtime to a small audience composed entirely of loyal unemployed actor friends.)

So, as he had many times before, Charles Paris decided he would stick with Maurice Skellern.

He thought of ringing his wife. Frances, headmistress of a girls' school, would still be on holiday. She had been away to Wales for a fortnight with their daughter, Juliet, son-in-law, Miles, and grandsons, Damian, Julian and Sebastian. Charles couldn't remember exactly when they were returning, but reckoned they must be back by now. Frances would need a few days to prepare for the new term. And, no doubt, to see her schools inspector.

The thought of this unknown figure, this David, hurt again. Most of the time he could shut it from his mind, just close off the part of his brain that controlled jealousy. But every now and then the pain seeped through.

He knew little about his "rival"—if that was the right word for his deserted wife's lover. He knew that David was married, and he knew that the affair was being conducted with elaborate secrecy. Indeed, its clandestine nature had provided a point of contact between Charles and Frances. They could laugh together at the ironies of the situation and he, more experienced in such deceits, could even give points of advice to his wife. So long as the relationship remained like that, so long as David remained firmly married, Charles could cope with it, contain it, shut out of his mind the details he did not want to know about.

But at their last meeting, for the first time since he had walked out on her, Frances had mentioned divorce. She had been unwilling to be pinned down to specifics, but the implication was clear that David finally intended to leave his wife and marry his mistress. After more than a year, the relationship had reached a new level of seriousness. And, for Charles, a new level of pain. While Frances was involved in the indignities and deceptions of an affair, he had not lost her; when she was actually married to someone else, he could no longer fool himself that he owned any part of her.

He wanted to talk to her, but was afraid to hear of any further advance in her plans to remarry, so he didn't dial the number of her Highgate flat.

For once Charles didn't meet any actors he recognized at the Unemployment Office, but he didn't let a detail like that stop him from going to the pub. After he had collected a pint, he saw a man along the bar who had been two ahead of him in the queue. He was in his thirties, dressed in a smart suit, very pale, and quickly downing a double scotch. Charles raised his glass amiably in salute and moved along the bar.

"Your first time, was it, signing on?"

The man gave a brief nod.

"Not an actor, are you?"

A slightly shocked shake of the head.

"What do you do then?"

"Until I was made redundant," the man said bitterly, "I was a sales manager for a firm making industrial plastics."

"Oh," said Charles.

"Now," the man continued dramatically, "I am nothing."

"Oh, don't take it so hard," said Charles. "Lots of people in the same boat."

"Oh yes," the man agreed, his voice thick with emotion, ". . . but the shame."

Charles provided further appropriate soothing. The encounter interested him. The recession had perhaps brought actors nearer to other workers, as more and more experienced the uncertainties of unemployment. In a world where nobody's job was secure, actors were no more vagabonds than anyone else.

That afternoon, as he dozed in his bedsitter, the payphone on the landing rang. It was a call he had been waiting for, not daring to hope for.

"Hello, Charles, it's Stan Fogden." The voice at the other end of the line was raucously Cockney.

"Yes?"

"Listen, you know we talked about you stepping in if someone dropped out?"

"Yes?"

"Well, it's happened. Phil suddenly got a telly."

"You mean—?"

"Yes, Charlie. The understudy's dream. You're on!"

They met in the Patisserie Valerie in Old Compton Street. Set in the middle of London's theatreland, it's a popular haunt of actors and actresses, who sit crowded on creaking wooden chairs, drink endless pots of tea, wolf cream cakes, browse through scripts, and gossip. Charles and Stan arrived around five o'clock, a busy time, as people working in the local theatres drop in for a snack before their day's duties start. There was a ten-minute wait before a table was free.

Stan eased his huge bulk down on to a defenceless chair. He was a Cockney actor in his forties, whose set of chins and matching stomach earned him a fairly regular living as television heavies, barmen, delivery men, taxi-drivers, bodyguards, removal men and so on. He had black hair that stuck out at odd angles and enormous good nature. If he had a fault, it was a tendency to overplay his role of lovable Cockney.

They ordered tea and eyed the plate of pastries. Stan picked up a large cream-filled slice and took a gargantuan bite.

"So," asked Charles, "what's the job?"

"Sure you can 'andle it?"

"Yes." (Never admit you can't do anything.)

"Well, look, set-up we got is this: the kind of A-Team is Bill Timmis and Phil, but Bill's got this three weeks on a feature in the Bahamas—all right for some, eh?—so I'm in for him, and now Phil's landed this telly. So, since the job's meant to start Wednesday, leaves me in a Loch."

One of Stan Fogden's supposedly endearing Cockney qualities was his constant use of rhyming slang. Some of it was familiar, but most was totally incomprehensible. Charles had a strong suspicion that Stan made it up, and had got used to asking patiently for glosses on the more obscure usages.

"Loch?"

"Loch Ness, Charlie—Mess."

"I see."

"So anyway, you'd be free? Haven't had the call from the Casting Directors at the National Theatre? Rachel Grant hasn't rung and asked you to give your King Lear?"

"Not this week, Stan."

"It'll come, it'll come."

"So what is the job?"

"It's a flat. Bloke wants a flat done."

The casual eavesdropper might have interpreted this as the planning of a burglary, but that was not the case. Nor was the job to which Stan referred a theatrical engagement. He, like many actors, dealt with his inevitable periods of "resting" by developing a sideline. In his case it was decorating.

"Is it complicated?" asked Charles, getting slightly cold feet about his skills as a decorator.

"Well, yes and no. I mean, there's quite a bit of paperhanging, but don't worry, that's my specialty. I'm hot stuff with the old pot of paste. All I'll want you to do is the Diana and the Jetpro."

"The what, Stan?" asked Charles patiently.

"Diana Ross—Gloss. Jet Propulsion—Emulsion."

"You do make them up, Stan."

"Absolute cobblers!" (Charles did know that one.) "Learnt 'em all at my mother's knee. Anyway, so I do the paperhanging, you do the paintwork, you know, and help out as and when. Reckon you can manage?"

"I think so. But what about . . . er . . . ?"

"Ah, you want to know about the Beesmake."

Charles wasn't sure whether or not that one was authentic, but he reckoned he could work it out. Bees Make Honey—Money.

"Well, yes."

"Right, the job's five hundred. We'll split fifty/fifty."

"That's very generous."

"Only way to do business, Charlie. Oh, one thing . . ."

"Yes?"

"Stumm about the money, okay?"

"Right."

"Don't want to make extra work for the taxman or the old DHSS, do we?"

"No. Don't worry. No one will ever know."

"Right."

"How long do you reckon the job'll take?"

"Hard to say, really. It's only basically four rooms. And the owner's away, so we can go at our own pace and move the stuff around. Don't know, week maybe . . ."

Two hundred and fifty quid for a week's work. Not a bad rate of pay for an actor. Many appearing on West End stages got less.

"And where is it?"

"Sort of Notting Hillish . . . 'Olland Park. The flat's over a restaurant. Called Tryst or something. D'you know it?"

"Yes," said Charles. "I do."

Chapter Three

ON THE TUESDAY evening, flushed with the confidence that he would soon have something coming in apart from his Unemployment Benefit, Charles decided to indulge in a little light drinking. Not too much, of course—he must have a steady hand for the gloss and emulsion in the morning—but just enough to make him feel comfortable.

The Montrose was a drinking club tucked away in a basement behind the Haymarket. The conversation that greeted anyone who pushed through its battered grey door left no doubt as to the profession of the majority of the club's clientele.

". . . I looked at Gemma and I could see, the line had just gone . . ."

". . . and the director says I must cut my hair, says it makes too much of a statement like this . . ."

". . . I said, 'For God's sake, Nigel, I'm through with playing funny vicars . . .'"

". . . I tell you, she couldn't direct a bicycle up a one-way street . . ."

Charles moved through the chorus of "I"s up to the bar and ordered a large Bell's whisky. When he was only going to have a couple of drinks, he'd have beer; when he intended to have more, he'd concentrate on the scotch. He drank more scotch than beer. Simply a matter of bladder-control, he told himself.

"How're things?" he asked the barman, whose name he could never remember.

"Pretty grim," came the lugubrious reply.

"Why?"

"Lease is coming up."

"What, the lease here? On the Montrose?"

The barman nodded. "And the block's been bought up by a new company who want us out."

"So the Montrose'll be closing."

"That's right."

"When?"

"End of the year."

"And isn't there any hope that . . . ?" Charles's words petered out as the barman shook his head.

The shock emptied the first large Bell's and another was quickly ordered. Holding it, Charles moved slowly across the crowded room.

It had been quite a body-blow. To lose the Montrose would upset his internal gyroscope. He'd been using the club for . . . how long? With a shock he realized it must be over fifteen years.

He had had too many such blows recently. Frances selling the family house in Muswell Hill and buying the flat. Frances taking up with her schools inspector. And now the Montrose . . . Next thing he'd be evicted from his Hereford Road bedsitter. Charles's world seemed to be crumbling around him. He felt every one of his fifty-five years. And, God, he was nearly fifty-six. He took a long, shuddering pull at the whisky.

"Charles Paris, isn't it?"

He focused on the woman from whom the voice came. Once before a chance encounter in the Montrose had started him on a bizarre adventure, the investigation of the death of Marius Steen. But that had been ten years earlier, and Jacqui, the girl he had met then, had been considerably younger than the woman who now confronted him.

This one was not unattractive, though the pinkish tinge to her brown eyes and the dark circles around them suggested he was not seeing her at her best. She was tall, almost Charles's height. Her brown hair had been cut short and not all its streaks of grey were due to the hairdresser's art. She was dressed in well-cut jeans and a floppy smock, but there was an air of untidiness about her, as if she had fallen asleep in a chair and just woken, dishevelled.

"Yes, you are Charles Paris," she repeated. "And you don't remember me."

It was embarrassingly true. She looked familiar, he was sure he had been thinking about her recently, but he couldn't put a name to her.

"Zoë Fratton," she said, without malice. "Don't you remember, we did a *Doctor Who* together."

33

She swayed, and Charles realized that he was talking to someone who was very drunk.

"That's right. Of course. Zoë Fratton. And we met when . . ." He changed the subject abruptly. "Let's sit down."

They squeezed their way on to one of the Montrose's tattily upholstered benches, but the move had not sufficiently obscured Charles's *faux pas*.

"I know what you were about to say," Zoë slurred. "You were about to say that we met a long time ago, while I was still married to that shit, Tristram Gowers."

Charles could not deny it.

"Before he went off with his pretty little bum-boy and left me stranded on the shore."

"Well—"

"That's what he did—just threw me over like I was something nasty his spade had turned up in the garden."

"I don't know the ins and outs of—"

"There are no ins and outs to know. That little French shit ruined a perfectly good marriage—that's all there is to it. Still . . ." A thought seemed to calm her. "Still, forget them. They're nothing. Finished. Out of my life. I've got new friends now. Friends who bring me bottles of gin." She held out her glass. "Have I got friends who'll buy me glasses of gin . . . ?"

She'd obviously had enough, but Charles didn't have the courage to refuse her. "Make it a large one," she called to his back as he went to the bar.

She looked shame-faced when he returned. "You're very kind, Charles. I'm sorry. I drink too much. Since Tristram went off, I . . . I'm sorry."

"Don't worry. I often feel the same. Cheers."

They clinked glasses.

"It's just so petty," said Zoë. "I feel myself getting old and embittered and alcoholic. Sometimes I'm frightened about the way I can behave. I do awful things, just awful . . ." She put a hand across her eyes, as if to wipe away some painful inner vision. "It's so horrible to feel yourself just eaten up with hatred. Not really hatred for Yves—he's not worth it, just a little tart. It's hatred for

34

Tristram. And I know hate is the other side of love. I think I still love him."

"It takes a long time for—"

"Yes, yes. You're being very kind, Charles. You're kind to listen to me. I know I'm behaving appallingly."

He could see the pain in her brown eyes, and feel the effort as she tried to claw her way back to self-respect.

"I'm not normally like this, Charles. It's just the weekend, knowing they were going off together yet again. The thought sort of made me mad. I just didn't feel responsible for myself at the weekend. I feel terrible about it."

Suddenly the tears came. Charles's proffered handkerchief was accepted and applied to her eyes. She shook her head firmly to demonstrate the return of control.

"I'm sorry about that. I'll stop now. Really." Her voice was firmer; there was even a hint of humour as she said, "It's just so pathetic—a grown woman torn apart by such a childish emotion as jealousy. That's all it is. I suppose I'm jealous of their money too, their success, the fact that they've made such a success of Tryst. Perhaps I could have coped better if things had been going well for me."

"Work?" asked Charles, seizing on a non-contentious subject of conversation.

"Yes."

"Nothing doing?"

"Nothing at all on the—" She stopped herself. "Do you know, I'm so used to saying that it's instinctive. As a matter of fact, a chance did come up this afternoon. Long chance, though. I'm sure I won't get it."

"What was it?"

"My agent rang after lunch. That's an event in itself."

"Same with mine."

"She'd been trying to get through all morning but—"

"Were you out?"

"What?" She paused. "No, I, er . . . the phone. The phone had just got knocked off, you know, the receiver . . . I didn't notice till after lunch."

"Ah. Well, what was the job?"

"Oh, be nice," she said wistfully. "Won't get it, though."

"Don't be so defeatist."

"No. Must think positive, mustn't I? The job is a week on a feature film in Tunisia."

"Starting when?"

"Next Monday. I am free, would you believe? But you know how last-minute features are. I rushed along to an interview this afternoon."

"How was it?"

She shook her head gloomily. "Don't think I did too well. There was another girl waiting who looked very glam. Sure she'll have got it. Still, nice to dream." She shook her head ruefully. "No, I'm sure I'll get the call tomorrow and I'll still be 'resting'. I wouldn't mind if 'resting' wasn't so bloody exhausting."

"We've all done our share."

"I think I've done more than my share. A bit of 'resting' out of drama school. 'Too tall,' they all said, 'you're too tall.' 'What about Vanessa Redgrave?' I said. 'She's tall. She's done all right.' 'Oh yes,' they said. 'Trouble is she's cornered the market in tall girls' parts. But don't worry, dear, you'll come into your own when you're older. Character parts, they'll be your forte.' So a few more years of 'resting'.

"Then, suddenly, it came right. Suddenly there *were* parts for me. In my early thirties I blossomed. I played principal boys, I did Noël Cowards, Shakespeares—I played Viola, Portia, Rosalind . . . And then it just seemed to go again. I was back to 'resting'. The fact that that coincided with the break-up of my marriage didn't help.

"And since then it's been—what? Bits and pieces, the odd day here, day there, nothing lasting. This should be my great time, showing off my forte in my forties. Where are all those wonderful character parts they promised me? No, I'm washed up. No doubt I've got a reputation for the booze, too. 'Thinking of booking Zoë Fratton? Ooh, I wouldn't, love. She's no good after lunch.' And that's all there is left of me."

She was silent and looked down into her glass. As if symbolically, it was empty. A slice of lemon clung precariously to the side.

"I'm sorry, Charles. I'm not always like this."

36

"I know." He believed her. Through all the maudlin self-hatred, there was something appealing about Zoë Fratton.

"It's just sometimes I feel so dreadful, as if I've done something awful. I feel so alone."

"We all do, Zoë." He rose. He had lost his taste for drinking. "I must go."

"Meet me here again, Charles," she pleaded urgently.

"All right," he said.

"Thursday?"

"Okay."

Stan Fogden had all the gear—brushes, ladders, pasting tables, lining paper, old newspapers, dust sheets. He kept it all in his "little Charlie" ("Charlie Chan—Van. Geddit, Charles?"), in which they drew up in the mews behind Tryst just before eight the next morning. It was an early hour for Charles, but Stan was a great believer in working "just like the professionals—because that's what we are, mate."

Charles had given some thought to what he should wear that morning. Obviously he needed old clothes for painting, but he was too much of an actor to wear just any old clothes. He had finally settled on a grey flannel shirt and a pair of shapeless tweed trousers. It was the costume he had worn in the role of a Communist poet in a play about the Spanish Civil War ("I would have welcomed the assassination of a President or anything else that curtailed this tedious piece"—*Huddersfield Daily Examiner*).

Since, as soon as they arrived, Stan handed Charles a huge pair of overalls that would cover everything, this attention to costume was rather wasted.

Tryst was set in that little hinterland of streets north of Holland Park Avenue. At the back it was made up of two mews cottages. The kitchen was in the garage part of one, with additional restaurant seating above. The other garage was used for Tristram Gowers' car, and above it was the flat in which he and Yves lived.

Both decorators were loaded with buckets and dust-sheets as they walked towards the entrance. One door led up to the flat; the other was the back way into the kitchen. Outside the flat door, propped against the wall, lay a plastic bag with the name of a Swiss Cottage butcher printed on the side. A rather nasty smell emanated from it.

Stan took a look inside. "Phew. Load of liver going off. Someone got the delivery wrong. Didn't know they was going away. That'll be pretty niffy by the time they get back, won't it?" He reached through the side of his overalls into his trouser pocket. "Now, out with the old fiddle."

"Don't tell me . . . Fiddle-dee-dee—Key?"

"You're learning, Charles my son. You most certainly are learning." Stan opened the door to the tiny hall. On the left another door led to the garage. Straight ahead was a staircase, carpeted in soft beige. "Up we go then. See what's to do. They was going to leave all the wallpaper and paint. They'd bought it. Be very pretty, I imagine. Did you know these two was a pair of soups?"

From the context Charles was pretty sure he knew what was meant, but he couldn't work it out. "Go on. I give up."

"Charles, I am disappointed in you. Soup Tureen—Queen."

They arrived on the landing and opened the door into the sitting-room. It was beautifully furnished and as spotless as Tristram's high standards would demand. Neatly in the middle of the carpet was a pile of paint tins and rolls of paper.

Stan knelt down. "I'll take a shufti at this lot. You go and see what's what in the Max."

"Sorry?"

Stan Fogden grinned triumphantly. "Maximum Headroom—Bedroom."

"Oh God," said Charles in mock exasperation as he crossed the landing and opened the door of the Max.

"Oh God," he said again, but this time it was a whisper of horror.

Splayed across the white bedspread lay the naked body of Yves Lafeu. Black blood had dried from the wounds in his throat and his mutilated genitals.

He was at least three days dead.

Chapter Four

WHILE STAN WAS phoning for the police, Charles hurried down the stairs of the mews cottage, seized with the thought of a new horror. The sight of Yves's bloody body had raised immediate and unsettling suspicions about the contents of the plastic bag outside the front door.

A cloud of flies dispersed as he approached it, seeming to lift the smell of decay up with them. As carefully as he dared, without making his inspection too apparent to any subsequent forensic investigator, Charles poked around in the nauseous contents of the bag.

With some relief he saw that it was only calves' liver. Three days in the sun hadn't made it a particularly salubrious package, but at least it did not contain any human remains.

Back in the mews, he was about to go upstairs when he thought of the garage. The door was not locked. He switched on the light to reveal emptiness.

Tristram Gowers' meticulously packed Volvo had gone.

The first of the police arrived in two squad cars with blue lights whirling, but by the end of the morning the mews yard was full of further marked and unmarked cars and vans. The predictable crowd of gawkers gathered on the periphery of the scene. Yves Lafeu's private moment of dying had suddenly become public property.

Charles and Stan were politely asked to wait in the restaurant until there was someone free to take statements from them. The sight of the slashed body had subdued even the Cockney's usual ebullience. He produced no rhyming formulae for murder. They sat in silence, Stan apparently engrossed in one of the old newspapers he had brought with him.

Charles looked around Tryst. Empty, and in daylight, the restaurant was drab and dusty, as if it had been closed for six months rather than three days. It was hard to remember how much life had been contained there on the Saturday evening. The atmosphere was as dead as that of a theatre the morning after a triumphant first night.

Charles looked across to the counter by the entrance and tried to visualize Monique Lafeu letting in the young man with blonded hair. He tried to see her brother swanning across the room to greet his friend, and Tristram appearing like an avenging fury from the kitchen. But the memory he raised was intellectual rather than cinematic. The only part of the scene he could recreate in his mind with clarity was the sound of Tristram's kitchen knife clattering down on to the bar counter.

He looked across there wistfully, but decided that swigging the Armagnac might not be the sort of thing the police would appreciate.

He felt uneasy and rather sick. The nausea arose partly from the recent shock of discovering Yves's body, but it had another cause as well. There were certain logical connections about the death which he was as yet unwilling to make. He didn't want to follow them through to their conclusion.

Stan stolidly did not look up from his paper as Charles rose and went up the brass-railed staircase to the upper dining-room. From there the whole mews could be seen except for its cul-de-sac end. Through the arch which provided the only access another police van was arriving as Charles looked. Tapes had been stretched between cones to provide a barrier and uniformed police opened these to admit the new vehicle, before returning to the job of convincing the curious crowd that there would be nothing to see and that they must have better things to do with their morning.

The side of the mews yard Charles faced backed on to a shopping parade. On street level were all the back-doors and delivery gates; above, a few windows, through which piles of boxes could be seen, suggesting that the first floors were store-rooms and offices rather than flats. The residential property was on Tryst's side of the mews, tarted-up and overpriced little cottages. On the previous Saturday night the shop premises would have presumably been empty. If there had been any witnesses of comings and goings to the mews in the early hours, they would have been Tristram and Yves's neighbours . . . or lovers sitting in parked cars in the mews . . . or passing vagrants . . .

Charles knew it was wishful thinking. After Tryst's diners and staff had left on the Saturday night, he felt fairly sure there was only one other significant event to witness—the departure from the garage of a Volvo containing one person.

The vast majority of murders, after all, are committed within the narrow confines of a close relationship.

"The police seem to have forgotten us," Charles observed, once again eyeing the well-stocked bar with yearning.

He only got a grunt from Stan, which was a measure of how deeply the Cockney had been shocked by what they had seen.

"Mind if I look at one of the papers?"

This was rewarded by a "Please yourself" shrug. Charles reached down and picked up one of the tabloids. Its news was sufficiently familiar for him to check the date. That Monday, two days previously. He settled down to pass the time.

Strange, he thought as he flicked through, how little news really stands the test of time. The initial shock of disasters fades, and increasingly the bulk of column space is filled with forecast and speculation, which are quickly rendered obsolete as real events overtake them. After two days, there was hardly anything left in the paper he was reading that seemed to have any relevance.

The exception he found in the gossip column. And that was only relevant because it added extra poignancy to the circumstances in which he found himself.

What caught his eye initially was a photograph of an extremely pretty girl. She was wearing a large hat, suggesting that perhaps the picture had been taken at a wedding, and her hair was longer, but Charles had no difficulty in recognizing the girl who had been introduced to him in that very room as "Henry".

The report confirmed it.

TV smoothie *Bertram Pride*, known to millions of adoring matrons as Philip Lexton, seems to have a new love in his life. The ageing juvenile obviously believes in the rejuvenating properties of youth (and maybe money), because he's gone for *Henrietta Rawsleigh*, 18-year-old daughter of "Bring Back The Rope" Tory MP, Sir Timothy Rawsleigh. Henry, as she's known to her Sloane Ranger chums, is apparently set on becoming an actress, so maybe the back-scratching with Bertram won't be completely one-sided. The couple, who've been seen together a few times in the last two weeks at London's nightspots, including Froggie's and Tryst, are keeping quiet about the connection. Neither was available for comment over the weekend, though there were strong rumours that they spent it together in Bertie's love-nest cottage in Kent, scene of many of his other conquests.

And since the subject of Tryst has come up, I'm afraid I have to report that Saturday night witnessed yet another of the public rows between the proprietors which contribute so much to the restaurant's unique ambiance.

The snide tone of the piece seemed doubly inappropriate to Charles as he sat in the melancholy silence of Tryst.

It was nearly mid-day when a plain-clothes Inspector and a uniformed constable finally came to take their statements. The Inspector was very apologetic for the delay, and, once he had started, very efficient in getting the details from them. Needless to say, he passed no comment on the murder, but something in his tone seemed to categorize it as a case that was finished, a case where the main outline had been defined and all that remained was the formal filling-in of the details.

Within an hour Charles and Stan were allowed to leave, warned that they might be required for supplementary questioning and that their appearance at an inquest might be necessary. They were thanked for their patience and assistance, and dismissed.

Stan's decorating equipment was neatly piled outside the front door of the mews cottage, and they were granted permission to take it away. The tapes were drawn back to allow the van to pass through, and they drove the gauntlet of curious stares of onlookers, who were no doubt fantasizing wildly about Charles and Stan's role in the proceedings.

Without asking, Stan drove back towards Hereford Road. He had turned left at the Notting Hill traffic lights before he spoke directly to Charles.

"Well," he said, "there's our five hundred quid up the sauer."

"Sauerkraut—Spout?" asked Charles automatically.

Stan nodded grimly. "If he's topped his boyfriend, I somehow don't see him wanting the flat decorated no more."

Charles didn't comment. He could hear the tension in Stan's voice. The apparent callousness was just his way of coping with the shock.

"I was glad that copper didn't ask nothing about how we was doing the job . . . you know, whether we was going to declare the loot or not."

"Oh, come on, Stan. He had more important crimes to think about than a little modest fiddling of the taxman."

"Yes, I suppose so. They unsettle me, though, any officials. It's their attitude of mind. Maybe they do all work for different organizations, but I reckon they're all hand in heavens."

Heavens Above—Glove. Charles had no problem with that one.

The van turned off Westbourne Grove into Hereford Road. "This is you, isn't it, Charlie?"

"That's right. Just up there on the right. Beyond the Volkswagen."

The van stopped outside the flaking frontage of what had once been a prosperous family house, but was now segmented into bedsitters. "Come in for a drink?" asked Charles. "I've got half a bottle of Bell's, if you—"

"No. Thanks all the same, Charles. Get back to the missus, I think. Feel quite shaken after that lot."

"Me too."

"Yeah. Well, look, if another decorating job comes up, I'll get in touch. Mel Ponting said he might want something doing—do you know Mel?"

"I seem to remember seeing credits for him a few years back, but not for some time."

"Ooh, Mel's not in the business any more. He's no fool. He's got a much better racket going."

But before Charles could ask what this "much better racket" was, Stan continued, "Anyway, I'll give him a bell and let you know. See you, Charlie. Sorry your introduction to the decorating business was a bit messy. Let's hope next time we don't find a lover's."

Charles was half-way up the stairs before he found a satisfactory explanation for it. Lover's Tiff—Stiff.

And he didn't feel very sure about that.

By the payphone on the landing there was a message scrawled by one of the interchangeable Swedish girls who occupied the other bedsitters in the house. Charles sometimes wondered why it was that every new tenant always turned out to be under thirty, female and Swedish (and, incidentally, built like a docker). He wove fantasies of an accommodation agency in somewhere unpronounceable like Jönköping, whose sole business was to stock this one house in Hereford Road. He waited the day, without much hope, when a Swedish man in a suit would knock on his door, offering him millions of kronor to move out and make the Scandinavian monopoly absolute. In more realistic moods he concluded that news of forthcoming vacancies was circulated by word of mouth from wench to strapping wench.

The messages they left for him contained such regular ambiguities that he thought they must be the result of perverseness rather than just unfamiliarity with the language. The current one read: "WRING WET DIANA VILSON", which a moment of thought translated into "RING WEST END TELEVISION – DANA WILSON."

No actor can contain the little surge of excitement which comes with a message to ring a producer or Casting Director. This always could be it, the Big One, the call that sets everything else in motion. Presumably Bertram Pride received such a call when he heard he'd got the part of Philip Lexton. Presumably every major success has started from one small call.

Dana Wilson's voice was so relaxed as to be almost inert. "Oh yes, Charles Paris. I met your agent at some reception. What was his name? Marcus Scotton . . . ?"

"Maurice Skellern."

"That's right. He was singing your praises like nobody's business."

"Was he?" That sounded most unlike Maurice. Charles found it difficult to imagine his agent as anything other than a voice at the end of a telephone, and even when he could give this image flesh, the idea of it going round lavishing praise on its client seemed mildly incongruous.

"Well, perhaps not that. He did say you'd done a couple of decent bits in your career."

Yes, that sounded much more like the Maurice Charles could visualize—reducing thirty-two years of work to "a couple of decent bits".

"Anyway, he seemed very keen on the idea of you coming along for a chat."

"Yes, fine."

"How's your availability at the moment?"

Trick question. Charles knew he must hold back the instinctive response. ("Not another solitary booking between here and the grave, so far as I can see. Even my promising sideline as a decorator has just been prematurely cut short by murder.") No, the skill was to imply interest, but not desperation; and to suggest that, by careful juggling, a few hours could be prised out of a busy schedule. He remembered with gratitude the line he had heard from Bertram Pride.

"Oh, a few things in the air," he replied casually, adding, "but can probably be shuffled around."

"How's this Friday for you?"

"Um . . ." Charles left a pause long enough for someone to summon up the image of a crowded diary before asking, "What sort of time?"

"Well . . ." Dana Wilson sounded less as if she were speaking than yawning. "There's a lunchtime fringe show I ought to get to, so I'd have to leave round twelve . . . then the afternoon looks a bit gummed up . . . got a half-past ten interview in the morning . . . how would round eleven do . . . ?"

"Ah." Charles's tone of voice implied a snag. "On the other hand . . ." No, the snag was perhaps not insuperable. "Yes, I shouldn't think he'd mind . . ." The "he" was meant to be some mythical American film producer. "Yes, I should think . . ." A moment's doubt cut this optimism short. "Hmm." The snag reared its head again. "Look, could we make it quarter past eleven? Then I'll be sure of making it." This suggested some early morning meeting of

45

enormous significance. The fact that all Charles would have to deal with on the Friday morning was the hurdle of getting out of bed did not matter; the "availability" game must be played according to the proper rules.

Dana Wilson bought it, anyway. "Yes, I think that'll be okay." And then, to ensure that she didn't lose any points and to reassert the enormous demands on her own time, she qualified her assent. "Might have to go to an outside rehearsal Friday morning, if the schedule on a drama we're doing gets changed. Long chance, but might happen, thought I should warn you. Anyway, I've got your number, so I'll let you know in good time if I have to cancel."

Honour was now satisfied on both sides.

"Oh, by the way," asked Charles, "is the interview for anything specific?"

"No, no, just general," drawled Dana and, after appropriate goodbyes, rang off.

Charles's question had not been unimportant. Actors like to know what part they're being considered for, simply so that they can choose their wardrobe and demeanour for the forthcoming interview. Young aspirants have turned up in spats and monocles to auditions for P. G. Wodehouse dramatizations. Casting for plays set in dockland brings out heavy denims and steel-toecapped boots. First World War dramas keep barbers busy doing the statutory short-back-and-sides. Beards and moustaches sprout and vanish on rumour of forthcoming parts; heads were shaved when a play about Buddhism was announced.

There is even a (surely apocryphal) story about the auditions for a new drama on the life of Abraham Lincoln. An actor who bore a slight likeness to the President read in *Stage* that the auditions would be held at a certain theatre a month from that date. He decided he would go all out for the part, growing the right sort of beard, hiring the right sort of costume, and reading so much about the character that by the day of the auditions he thought he *was* Abraham Lincoln. When he arrived at the theatre, he was assassinated.

Charles Paris adjusted his appearance according to the part for which he was being considered, but nowadays he did not make his metamorphoses too extreme. On one occasion he had gone to an audition for Jean Anouilh's play about the martyred Archbishop of Canterbury, *Becket*. Due to a misunderstanding by Maurice Skellern, Charles had arrived expecting to read for Samuel Beckett's *Waiting for Godot*, and had therefore dressed as a tramp.

He still felt shaken by the morning's events and it was with difficulty that he restrained himself from hitting the whisky bottle until half-past five. The fact that the pubs were then open made him feel almost righteous about pouring a couple of inches into a tumbler. But just as he raised the drink to his lips, the telephone on the landing rang.

It was Kevin O'Rourke.

"Charles. Have you heard about Yves?"

Charles explained the harsh circumstances in which the news had been broken to him.

"Oh, my God. Listen, Bartlemas and I are in a terrible state about it. And about Tristram . . . Where on earth is Tristram?"

"His car had gone from the garage."

"Oh, no. Charles, do you think you could come round?"

Bartlemas and O'Rourke lived in Ideal Road, Islington, in a four-storey Victorian house, which inside was a shrine to their two idols, Kean and Macready. The walls were hung with prints and playbills; on every horizontal surface clustered statuettes, hats, swords, rings and other props; bookcases were tight with leather-bound volumes of biographies and memoirs.

Charles had been to the house for a good few convivial evenings over the years, but on this occasion the atmosphere was subdued. William Bartlemas and Kevin O'Rourke were, as ever, dressed alike, but the sober black trousers and charcoal pullovers did not draw attention to their livery. Bartlemas was sympathetic to his friend, but O'Rourke was clearly the one who was suffering most.

"It's terrible, Charles . . ."

"Terrible . . ." Bartlemas echoed supportively.

"We only saw it in the paper this afternoon . . ."

"And at first we just couldn't believe it . . ."

"To think of Yves being dead . . ."

"I mean, he was so beautiful, and so alive . . ."

"Yes, wicked sometimes, but so alive . . ."

"The paper implied it was murder . . ."

"There weren't many details, but . . ."

"Do you think they could be wrong? Do you think perhaps it wasn't murder . . . ?"

Charles shook his head sadly. "I'm sorry. I'm afraid there is no question about it."

He was glad they accepted that. He could have elaborated, but would rather have spared their feelings, and his own, by not re-creating the bloody tableau he had seen that morning.

"They're bound to blame Tristram," said O'Rourke with sudden bitterness.

"Bound to . . ." Bartlemas agreed.

"Well, you can see their point." Charles made his voice as level and reasonable as he could. "In any murder case the first suspect is always the victim's cohabitant. And we all witnessed Tristram threatening Yves with the knife."

"Yes, but that was just part of their relationship. Yves was always a bit of a tart, always being unfaithful, always hurting Tristram, but that was part of his charm. Tristram would never have killed him . . ."

"Not just for *that*, no . . ."

"We don't know the full background," said Charles judiciously. "The arrival of that boy at the restaurant on Saturday night may have been the culmination of a long quarrel. Perhaps it was just the final straw. It made Tristram see red and—"

"Oh, for God's sake!" O'Rourke broke in with uncharacteristic anger. "Tristram wasn't like that. He was quite sane. Everyone seems to think just because a person's gay, he lives life on a permanent emotional knife-edge."

"Now, I didn't say—"

"No, you didn't, but you were moving in that direction. And I'm sure that's what the police are thinking. 'Oh well, if it's a gay couple, they must be at each other's throats all the time. It must be the lover who did it.'"

Charles didn't mention the attitude of the Inspector who had taken his statement, though it might very well have reflected the sort of views O'Rourke described. "Listen, I know you're fond of Tristram—"

"Of course I'm fond of him. He's my nearest relative, apart from anything else. And round the time that he 'came out', when he was very confused, we saw a lot of each other and got very close."

"I'm sure you did," said Charles gently. "But you must see, just from the point of view of ordinary logic, that Tristram is the obvious suspect."

O'Rourke's silence conceded this point.

"I mean, it'd be different if he was around to defend himself. But the fact that both he and his car are missing does look like an admission of guilt."

"That's certainly how the police are taking it." The new bitterness in O'Rourke's voice seemed temporarily to have silenced Bartlemas's echoes.

"Have you spoken to the police?" asked Charles.

"Yes, of course I have. Tristram's my cousin. I have a right to know what's going on."

"What did they say?"

"They were pretty non-committal. They confirmed that Yves was dead and that 'foul play' was suspected. They also confirmed that Tristram was missing."

"Nothing else?"

"They said that enquiries were under way, and they would keep me informed of appropriate developments."

"Meaning?"

"Meaning very little, I imagine. Meaning that, so far as they're concerned, another pooftah's done in his lover and the world is probably a better place without him."

The depth of resentment in O'Rourke's tone spoke of a long history of persecution. Charles was a little surprised to hear it. He had known Bartlemas and O'Rourke for so long that he had almost forgotten they were gay.

He maintained his tone of moderation. "I don't know whether they are as prejudiced as you think or not, but suspecting Tristram of the murder is a fairly natural reaction. I mean, do you have any alternative thesis to put forward?"

O'Rourke gave a short shake of his head.

"Well, I'm afraid, until Tristram turns up to clear his name, he's bound to remain the Number One suspect."

Tristram Gowers didn't turn up. But his car did.

To Charles's surprise, the police were as good as their word to Kevin O'Rourke. They did ring to keep him informed of appropriate developments.

The enquiry had taken on an international aspect. The French police, at the request of Scotland Yard, had investigated the house at Mas-de-Pouzard.

Outside it they had found Tristram Gowers' Volvo, all packed up for the holiday.

Of the vehicle's owner there was, as yet, no trace.

Chapter Five

"THE THING I want to know, Stan, is how was the job set up?"

"What—decorating Tryst?"

"That's right."

"Well, the owner set it up. One who's disappeared. Him with the Irish."

Irish Jig—Wig. Charles knew that one; it was authentic, traditional rhyming slang, not one of Stan's more dubious coinings.

"What, he rang you?"

"No, no. Remember, I'm only Bill Timmis's understudy. Someone must've recommended Bill to him, but Bill couldn't do it because of his Bahamas job, so he put the bloke on to Phil, but Phil'd just heard about his telly, so Phil put him on to me."

"I see. When were the arrangements made?"

"Ooh, two weeks back, I reckon."

"You see, I was wondering why the job was set up to start on the Wednesday. Tristram and Yves were meant to leave on the Sunday morning, so the decorators could have moved in on the Monday . . . unless Tristram actually wanted the delay . . . unless he didn't want Yves's body to be discovered for three days, which would give him time to make his getaway."

Charles sat back, rather pleased with the way he had worked that out, but looked up to see Stan shaking his head with pity.

"Doesn't work, Charlie. Number One: I asked for it to start on the Wednesday. I was doing a job down at Teddington . . ."

"What—with Thames Television?"

"No, no. Vinyl wallpaper on a kitchen, bathroom and toilet. And I reckoned it'd take me longer than it did. I worked evenings and finished end of last week."

"So why didn't you start doing Tryst on Monday?"

"Two reasons. I hadn't got you set up for a start."

"Oh, that's true."

"*And* I didn't know when old Tristram and his mate was actually leaving. I'd said I couldn't start till the Wednesday and he said, 'Oh, fine, we'll be away by then.'"

"I see."

"But, Charlie," Stan continued inexorably, "there is another flaw in your logic. If you're trying to work out some theory that Tristram Whatnot set this whole murder up in advance, then you're way off beam."

"Why?"

"Oh, come on, Charles. Use your Michael."

"Er?"

"Michael Caine—Brain. Look, if Tristram was planning to top the Frog, he chose a pretty peculiar way of doing it. Immediately he makes himself the main suspect and pisses off to France. Now there's no way he can come back here after that, is there?"

"No."

"So, if he knew he wasn't coming back, why the hell did he arrange to have the restaurant redecorated?"

Charles couldn't answer that. He had occasionally prided himself on some ability as a detective, but now he felt he was being given a lesson in the basics.

"What it means is," Stan continued, making Charles feel even smaller, "that, if you think old Tristram done it, then it has to be a spur-of-the-moment job. Sudden blaze of anger, out with the old knife—" he drew a finger across his throat with an unpleasantly guttural sound, "—and get the hell away as soon as possible."

"What it also means," said Charles slowly, "is that if you think somebody else did it—"

"And you'd have to be a bit of a loony to think that."

"Maybe," Charles conceded. "But, if somebody else did do it, they might not have known about the decorating, and they might have thought it would be a month before anyone would go into the flat and find the body."

Once again his optimistic look was met by a pitying gaze from Stan.

"And what, meanwhile, does this other bloke who done it do with Tristram?"

"Ah," said Charles. "I hadn't thought of that."

"Charlie, my son, you're really a bit of a prat."

That wasn't rhyming slang, but Charles knew exactly what it meant. "Another beer, Stan?" he asked, picking up their two glasses.

When Charles came back from the bar, Stan had been joined by a thin man with a sharp face, who, in spite of his greying hair, managed to look like a naughty schoolboy, a sort of grown-up Artful Dodger.

"Charlie—this is Mel Ponting, who I told you about."

"Hi. What can I get you to drink?"

"Oh, vodka Campari, please."

"It only took me a couple of years in the business," Mel Ponting announced when they were all supplied with drinks and sitting round the table, "to realize that acting was a mug's game. I mean, I done all right, got a few good tellies, that sort of thing, but I got this feeling I wasn't maximizing my potential. I mean, it doesn't take many weeks of 'resting' for you to twig that you ain't got any money coming in."

Charles and Stan smiled condescendingly at this truism. "But that's just part of the business," said Charles.

"Well, that was the part I wasn't going to put up with. I grew up in the East End, and all my mates, they was earning money. When they hadn't got work, they made work. As an actor you can't do that—you got to wait till some berk employs you. Well, I'm not good at waiting.

"So, anyway, I looked around at all the actors I knew and almost everywhere I saw the same thing—people being under-used, spare capacity going to waste. Now any businessman'll tell you what you got to do is make sure that you're using everything you got all the time—that's the way to productivity. So I saw all these actors, and I knew they had a lot of potential. I just had to harness that potential. I had to find a market for all the energy they was wasting while they wasn't in work."

"So what did you do?"

"Well, my first thought was to make more work for them, actually get things going myself, go into production. I did that for a few years, put on a few shows, made a few bob, but it wasn't what I was after. All risks and hassles, that business. As a producer, you're damned nearly as exposed as an actor. So I give that up.

"Then I tried agency. All right, one actor on his own can't keep in work all the time, but if you're drawing on a whole stable of actors,

53

well, you spread your risk and you ought to be able to survive. All right, I proved you can. Survive. Wouldn't put it a lot higher than that. Shall I tell you what the trouble is? As an agent, you're only on ten per cent. Okay, you can push it up to fifteen, but it still ain't princely. You see, you're still dependent on the same berks who wouldn't employ you as an actor, and at any given time, half your stock—you know, the actors you got on your books—are doing bugger all.

"And then it come to me. I realized where I was going wrong. I saw the light—like Paul on the road to Singapore . . . or was it Bob Hope on the road to Morocco? I realized that in a profession where most of the people are out of work most of the time, it's daft to try and make money out of that small slice of their time while they're actually working. What you got to do is make your money out of the time they aren't working. And that's how Actors Anonymous was born."

"I'm afraid I've never heard of it," Charles confessed.

"Well, of course you haven't. That's why they're Anonymous—no one knows who they are. Anyway, I like to keep a kind of low profile, publicity-wise, because I don't want to draw the Inland Revenue's attention to what I'm doing."

"So what are you doing?"

"Basically, I supply actors wherever they're needed. That is, wherever they're needed outside of show-business. You'd be surprised how often someone's glad of an actor round the house or in the office."

"But what sort of things do they *do*?"

"Well, all right, the basic stuff's domestic."

"What, you mean the old charring?"

"Yes. Domestic cleaning, waiting, serving behind bars—that's the basic turnover of the business. It's also the official bit—that's the stuff that goes through the books. Davenport Domestics that side's called. But it's only the tip of the iceberg, you know. Lots of other things Actors Anonymous do."

"Like?"

"Well, sticking with the domestic, we can do the Rolls-Royce service. That's really butlers and parlour-maids. Surprising how popular they are to add a bit of snob value to the old suburban dinner party."

"But I thought butlers had years of training and—"

"Listen, Charles, how many actors do you know who haven't played a butler at one time or another in their career? Go on, how many?"

"Well . . ."

"Anyone who's done rep has been in God knows how many tatty old thrillers in which the butler at least might have done it. There's butlers and maids in hundreds of plays. And, as long as television keeps churning out all these Victorian and Edwardian series, new butlers are being trained every day. A series like *Upstairs, Downstairs* is like a blooming university course."

"But do they really know enough to convince the—"

"For one evening, Charles, they can busk it. Go on, how many actors have you known go on stage without knowing their lines?"

"A good few."

"Right. And yet they don't dry, do they? They keep going, they get through. Any actor worth his salt can be a totally convincing butler for one evening."

Charles laughed. "You said it wasn't just domestic stuff."

"No. Once you get the idea, all kinds of other things follow. I mean, back to our suburban dinner party. All right, you got the staff sorted out, trouble is the hosts have the most unbelievably boring friends. But if you throw in a couple of actors, playing a . . . what shall we say? . . . a Detective-Inspector and a poet, well, things may start to hum a little."

"It'd never work. They'd never sustain it."

"It has been done, Charles. You take my word, it has been done. Not often, but it worked."

"But you'd have to know so much about—"

"You don't need a lot for an evening. And every actor's played a Detective-Inspector at some stage or other—in all the thrillers where he wasn't playing the butler.

"But now I get more exotic requests, you know. Had a few bookings for blokes to appear as long-lost boy-friends to break up affairs that weren't working. Well, saves a 'Dear John' letter. Then I had a good one last year from a bloke who was in the Scrubs doing seven years for his part in a mail-snatch. He'd got this boy at public school and he wanted me to provide a respectable pair of parents for Speech Day, you know, to keep up his son's image. I found a couple who did that lovely—just played the same parts in *The Browning Version* in rep.

"Had another good one recently. Bit different. Request from a fairly big firm that was getting worried about productivity levels. You know, they thought the staff was getting lazy, taking too long lunch-breaks, that sort of number . . . So they come to me and ask if I've got a couple of actors who can spend a week in the place pretending to be Management Consultants. No problem. I give them a good briefing, tell them how they've got to keep asking everyone how many people there are in each department, and use a lot of phrases like 'staff redeployment', 'redundancy levels' and 'early retirement' and that's all there is to it. Worked a treat. The firm was delighted. Everyone pulled their socks up, productivity soared. And, of course, the firm saved thousands. I mean, I charged plenty for the two actors, but that's about one per cent of what real Management Consultants would have cost. No, Actors Anonymous is really booming, and you know I get the feeling I'm only scraping the surface of the market."

"And you take an agency fee for all this?"

"That's right. Twenty per cent because I've got the contacts."

"But surely some of the actors get recognized?"

"Very rarely, Charles. Trouble with all you Thespians is you think the world has only got eyes for you, think no one notices anyone else in the room. Not true, I'm afraid, my son. Anyway, it's a matter of context. If you go to a party and someone's pointed out to you as the butler, you tend to accept that at face value. You don't go staring at him and thinking, 'Didn't I once see you giving your Malvolio at Hornchurch?' Even if the bloke does look vaguely familiar, so what? There's enough actors who've given up the unequal struggle and gone into other businesses, aren't there?"

"True enough."

Mel Ponting grinned. "I reckon old Stan here's sometimes in two minds about giving it all up and concentrating on the decorating."

"Do sometimes think about it, yeah. I mean, if I've just spent a couple of days on a telly with one of those young directors who thinks he's Cecil B. De Mille, I'd give anything to get back to the old wallpaper brush."

"Yes, but, Mel," Charles insisted, "what happens if one of your domestics really gets a big break, suddenly becomes a household name? You can't send him out charring then, can you?"

"Well, no, but no successes happen like literally overnight. There's always a bit of a time-lag. Anyway, with that sort of break, the bloke probably doesn't need the money from the charring so he gives it up naturally. Mind you," Mel added, with a shrewd tap of the finger to his nose, "I don't lose out that way. A lot of them, when they become big stars, they want staff themselves. They're loyal, they know me, so I get bookings for other actors to go and clean for them. I mean, I done that for Bernard Walton."

"What, he used to char for you?"

"You bet. Don't mention it when you see him—bit sensitive about it—but he did. And Bertram Pride, and all. Whole lot of them. And now they've made it, I provide their staff. It's a nice self-generating business I got going, Charles."

"Sounds like it. But don't you ever hanker to get back on the stage?"

This suggestion got a derisive snort. "You have got to be joking." Then Mel Ponting's tone became brisk and businesslike. "Anyway, do you want to get on the books, Charles?"

"Well . . ."

"That's why Stan fixed up this introduction."

"Yes."

"I gather the old decorating's a bit quiet right now. Last job came to a bit of a sticky end, didn't it?"

"You could say that." Charles winced at the memory. "Well, yes, I'd like to have a go. I just wonder whether I've got the abilities to—"

"Charles," asked Mel patiently, "have you ever played a butler?"

"Of course. Lots of times. The *Eastern Daily Press* described my butler in *Arsenic For Two* as 'to the manner born'."

"See. What about barmen?"

"God. Story of my television career, barmen. I even played one for a whole series called *The Strutters* . . . well, the series was never completed, but . . . And then, when I was a barman in some

57

incomprehensible *Play For Today*, the *Observer* said I was 'lugubriously efficient'."

"Well, that's all you need to be, isn't it?"

"Mind you, I've never played a char. Those parts are always monopolized by lovable Cockney ladies."

"Yes, but everyone knows how to Hoover and dust."

"Hmm. Don't think my bedsitter would be much of an advertisement for my talents."

"I didn't say everyone *did* it; I said everyone *knows how* to do it. Anyway, you can do most things when you're being paid for them."

Charles nodded, in full agreement with that sentiment.

"Right. You're on the books of Actors Anonymous, as of today."

"Great."

"Can't promise anything straight away, but things will come up, you take my word." Mel suddenly looked cautious. "Oh, and . . ."

"Yes?"

"I can trust your discretion in not mentioning any of our mutual activities to the taxman, can't I?"

Charles's expression was deeply pained. "Mel, what do you take me for?"

"Fine. Sorry. Had to ask. Do come across the odd nut in this business, you know. Right, so that's it." Mel Ponting drained the last of his vodka Campari and rose. "Back to the office. Thanks for the drink. Oh, and, Charles . . ."

"Yes?"

"Don't ring me, I'll ring you. Okay?"

Charles had been in two minds about going to the Montrose on the Thursday evening. After the collapse of his financial hopes from the decorating job at Tryst, he knew that he shouldn't really afford another evening's drinking. But, though that particular door had closed, Mel Ponting had opened another at least a little, and Charles felt he could take the risk. His attitude to money always hovered between two extremes. When he had no prospects of anything coming in, he felt despairingly poor; but it only needed a hint of a rumour of a prospect for him to imagine the money already in the bank. And to spend it accordingly.

He had not forgotten his vague arrangement to meet Zoë Fratton at the club, but, after the events at Tryst, he had discounted the possibility of her turning up. However inimical her relationship was with her ex-husband, she was bound to be affected by his disappearance after apparently committing a murder. And, apart from her emotional state, she was likely to be occupied with questioning, as the police tried to establish Tristram's whereabouts.

He was therefore surprised to see Zoë ensconced in a corner when he eased his way through the theatrical crush at the Montrose at nine o'clock that evening. He was almost more surprised to see that sitting beside her was Bertram Pride.

"Can I get you a drink?" asked Charles, gesturing with his own large Bell's.

"No, thanks. Bertram's just got us one." As on the last occasion, her voice was slurred, suggesting that the gin and tonic she clutched was not her first of the evening. "Do you two know each other?"

"We met . . . recently . . ."

"Yes, Saturday, wasn't it?" Neither of them wanted to mention where they had met.

But Zoë herself brought up the fateful word. "You heard about events at Tryst, Charles?"

"Yes." He didn't elaborate. If she didn't know about his discovery of the body, there was no need to draw her attention to it. She looked in a very tense state; he didn't want to do anything to aggravate her condition.

She appeared not to know of his involvement; at any rate, she didn't mention it. "I'm lucky," she said, "to have good friends. Bertram came round when he heard. He knew I'd be upset."

Bertram Pride gave a self-depreciating dip of his head at the compliment. "Just glad if I can be any help."

"Oh, but you *were*," asserted Zoë. "He brought me another bottle of gin, Charles. Certainly knows the way to a girl's heart."

She let out a little giggle, but there wasn't a lot of humour in it. "Good to have friends who're loyal, when things are bad. Bertram and I worked together in rep . . . Bromley. He knew I'd be upset. Doesn't forget his old friends, just because he's a big star."

Bertram Pride gave a little, embarrassed grin, as Zoë continued,

"And I've got you too, Charles, you coming to support me in my hour of need." Her voice gave a little, hiccoughing lurch. "Or do I mean my hour of triumph?"

She smiled at their blank expressions. "Don't you understand, Yves Lafeu is dead. And, so far as the world's concerned, Tristram killed him. Wouldn't you call that two birds with one stone?"

"What do you mean—'as far as the world's concerned'?" asked Charles gently.

Zoë looked flustered. "Well, I don't mean anything. I mean, Tristram must have done it, mustn't he? There isn't anything else to think, is there?"

"No," said Bertram soothingly. He was watching her very carefully, as if worried about her mental state.

"Have you had long sessions with the police?" asked Charles.

"Long? Yes, long, long sessions. I have had long sessions with the police. Their view is . . ." her voice was suddenly more sober, "that I will not see Tristram again."

"You mean they think he's committed suicide?"

She nodded with too much emphasis. "That is exactly what they think. They've sent a team to France to investigate. Their view is . . ." she repeated the words with fastidious care, "that dear Tristram's body is likely to turn up in the River Lot."

"Well, I suppose that might be a logical conclusion," said Bertram.

"Oh yes. For years I've wanted both of them dead, dreamed about it, been obsessed by the idea, and now it's happened . . ." her voice broke, "I can't cope."

Both men leaned forward to take her hands, and murmur reassurances about it just being shock and her soon feeling better and all the other insufficient platitudes that are produced in times of stress.

"I know it's difficult," said Charles, "but you've really got to try to think beyond this, think of the rest of your life." Then, remembering something that might cheer her, he asked, "Oh, what happened about that job in Tunisia? You never told me about that."

Unfortunately, that subject was not calculated to improve her mood. "I heard from the Casting Director. No. It's gone to the other girl."

"I'm sorry."

"Was that the job you mentioned when I rang you Wednesday morning?" asked Bertram.

"Yes. I was all excited about it then. Ten minutes later I heard I hadn't got it."

"Bad luck." Bertram looked genuinely upset by the news. Charles decided he would have to revise his opinion of the star. He had been inclined to dismiss Bertram as just another smoothie, but was impressed by the depth of sympathy Zoë was receiving.

"Wednesday," she went on bitterly, "was not a good day. First that news, and in the afternoon the police."

"I'm sorry," Charles repeated, again inadequately.

Bertram Pride looked at his watch. "I'm afraid I've got to be off. I really just dropped by to the flat for a quick chat, Zoë, and I'm running a bit behind . . ."

"Of course. No, I'm very grateful. Sorry to have kept you. I do appreciate what you've done." Zoë Fratton rose with surprising grace to embrace her friend. She was almost as tall as he was and they made an impressive couple. "You have been most provident in peril."

Bertram smiled at some private joke. Charles thought the reference was probably a quotation, but he couldn't identify it. The conversation of actors who have worked together is frequently littered with incomprehensible allusions to productions long forgotten.

"You'll be all right with Charles," said Bertram reassuringly, passing over the baton of responsibility.

Charles discharged his duty well. After a couple more drinks, he steered Zoë out to a taxi, and accompanied her to her flat in a rather grim block round the back of John Barnes department store off the Finchley Road.

Inside her dark hall, she suddenly put her arms round him. "You've been so kind to me, Charles. I don't deserve it."

"Of course you do," he said, as if patting a dog.

"I've done awful things. I've thought awful things. I'm not a good person."

The tensions in her body squeezed him closer to her. His own body, with its usual appalling sense of timing, responded physically.

61

Zoë observed this, and looked at him closely, with a half-smile. "No, I don't think it's quite the moment for me to expose my varicose veins to you."

"No, I didn't mean . . ." Charles gently disengaged himself.

"Oh, you probably did. Quite flattering, you know, when you get to my age."

Charles blushed.

"And who knows," Zoë continued, giving him a little ginny kiss, "the day may come . . ." Her mood darkened suddenly. "But not now. Not till all this is sorted out, till the police have consigned the file to their archives. At the moment there's too much tension, too much suspicion."

Charles moved to the door. "Are you sure you'll be all right here on your own?" he asked, wishing as soon as the words were out of his mouth that he'd rephrased them. The question sounded too much as if he were suggesting he should stay.

But fortunately Zoë didn't take it that way. "No, I'll be all right," she assured him.

Charles said his goodbyes. Just before the door closed behind him, he heard Zoë, with a strange, cracked laugh in her voice, announce, "I wanted the pair of them dead. And now I've got what I wanted."

Chapter Six

THE LANGUOR OF Dana Wilson in the flesh matched that of her telephone manner. She was small, with hooded sleepy blue eyes which were surrounded by shiny reddish make-up. She had that good grooming which seems to be obligatory for women in television—hair recently styled with a couple of pinkish streaks, loose flowered blouse and revivalist miniskirt. She seemed to be having difficulty in summoning up much interest in Charles Paris.

"Of course, we haven't got a great deal in production at the moment," she admitted drowsily.

"Yes, Maurice said this would just be a general interview."

"Maurice?"

"My agent."

"Oh yes. Of course, we have done some wonderful productions. Some of the casting in our big series has been just inspired."

"Yes," Charles agreed patiently. It came back to him that everyone in television always attributed success to the contribution of their own particular department. Failure was, of course, due to the shortcomings of all the other departments.

"I mean, I myself actually cast *Lexton and Sons* . . ."

She left a pause which Charles filled with an appropriately impressed "Really?"

"One of my first big assignments. Before that I was secretary to Tilly Lake. Do you know Tilly?"

"Yes, she cast *The Strutters*, which I was in."

"Oh, you've worked for WET, have you?"

"Yes." God, she hadn't even made the effort to check in the company index to see whether Charles had a record card or not.

"Of course, Tilly's mostly Light Ent.," said Dana, with the contempt all Drama Departments always demonstrate for their more frivolous and popular rival.

"Yes."

There was a languid pause. Charles decided he had better volunteer some of the information he would have expected her to ask for. "I didn't bring any photographs or cuttings, because I never think they mean a lot."

"Oh, don't you?" This idea seemed to elicit a tiny spark of interest.

"No. Do you?"

"No, not really." She slumped back into inertia.

"But perhaps you'd like me to tell you some of the things I've done . . . ?"

"Oh, I don't think so," Dana replied, as if he were suggesting some enormous imposition. "No, I'm very much a *face* person."

"Oh."

"I see a face, and I lock it away in my mind—I have a photographic memory, you know—and then, maybe weeks, maybe months, maybe years later, I see a script and I see a part, and a face rises to the surface of my mind."

"I see," said Charles with proper awe for this mystic approach to the business of casting. "But perhaps if I were to tell you the sort of parts I've played in the past, you might—"

"Oh, I don't think that'll be necessary. I've got your face locked in my mind."

Charles felt tempted to ask whether he should leave, since the important part of the interview seemed to have been achieved, but he held back. That seemed to suit Dana well; she wanted a passive audience for her monologue of self-congratulation.

"When I saw the first scripts for *Lexton and Sons*, I just knew their faces instinctively. It's a knack, you know." She condescended this information to Charles as a mere mortal. "I knew that Millicent had to be Rita Lexton, and of course George was born to play Walter. Then Hilary was a natural for Gilda . . ."

"And Bertram Pride for Philip," Charles supplied, in the hope of speeding up her somewhat torpid delivery.

Her face clouded. "Well, yes. Actually, someone else suggested Bertram. I had another idea, but, well . . ." She shrugged. "Sometimes we all have to bow to *force majeur*, don't we?"

"Yes." Charles made another attempt to bring the conversation round to his own work. "I have done television drama, you know. It hasn't all been Light Ent."

"Oh." Dana spoke dreamily, not hearing him. "I have discovered some very major stars, you know, or people who could have been. Do you know Wally Gammons . . . ?

"Know the name."

"I gave him his start."

"Really?"

"And Frank Stillman—such a sweetie, Frank . . . And Martin Sabine—do you know him?"

"Again, the name . . ."

"Of course, he just does radio now. Tragic, that. And then there's Valeta Chambers . . ."

As the catalogue continued, Charles remembered another fact about people in television—*they all discovered everyone*. Any successful name that's mentioned immediately prompts a sequence of claims from those who "gave him his first break".

Charles wondered why the interview with Dana Wilson had been set up. Then, on reflection, he realized that it was absolutely typical of Maurice Skellern. His agent's eternal instinct was to do nothing, but every now and then he would sense the client's unease was building to the point of separation, and he would make a gesture. He would be seen to do something on his client's behalf. The fact that these gestures were invariably useless did not matter. The client felt obscurely reassured, convinced that in his own special way Maurice really was rooting for him. Charles's current interview at WET, he reflected, was a perfect demonstration of the Skellern technique.

He was getting bored with Dana Wilson's listing of her discoveries, but he didn't feel he should interrupt. Though the prospects didn't at the moment seem promising, there might come a day when he would be glad of the Casting Director's goodwill. An optimist, after all, might conclude that his face was already locked in the filing cabinet of her mind, just waiting to be matched with the right script, after which the name of Charles Paris would join the roll of honour Dana Wilson was so laboriously reciting. But Charles Paris was not an optimist.

Relief came when the phone on Dana's desk rang. Apparently it was her secretary ringing from the outer office.

"Yes. All right. Could you ask her to wait? I'm nearly through."

The Casting Director put the phone down and smiled wearily at

Charles. "Well, it's been most interesting to hear about your work . . ."

What? But I haven't told you anything.

"And I do assure you that I will bear you in mind, and when the right sort of part comes up . . ."

Oh yes, heard that before.

"I've got all the details of your agent . . . Marcus—"

"Maurice Skellern."

"Yes." The weariness of her smile was now melting into long-suffering.

Charles decided he could risk a straight question. "Are you actually casting anything at the moment?"

Dana Wilson looked pained by this lapse of etiquette. "Well, there have been production cutbacks . . . I mean, with the funding of Channel Four, the company's resources are stretched and—"

Having breached the wall of good manners, Charles felt he had nothing to lose by pressing on. "Yes, but are you actually casting anything?"

"Well, there is a big new drama series currently under consideration, in which I would almost certainly be involved . . ."

"And when's that scheduled in the studio?"

This did unsettle her torpor a little. "Well, it's not confirmed yet, but it's hoped that December . . . certainly early next year . . ."

Good God, and until then she would have no work, just come into the office, sit through any number of tedious interviews of the kind she had just conducted, go to a few theatres in the evenings, chat with her colleagues . . . Not for the first time, Charles was aware of the huge gulf between himself and people in full-time employment. When they had nothing to do, they still got paid; when he had nothing to do, he didn't. On the other hand, when he thought of the idea of killing time for six months in WET House, he knew he wouldn't have changed places.

He instantly recognized the girl who sat in Dana Wilson's outer office. Not only had he been introduced to her within the last week, he had also seen her photograph in the newspaper. "It's Henry, isn't it?"

The huge blue eyes widened even further as she struggled for a second to place him. Fortunately she got to his name before he had to prompt her. "Charles Paris?"

"Yes."

"We met at Tryst, where that frightful . . . thing happened."

"Yes. With Bertram."

She blushed. "That's right."

They stood awkwardly in silence. The phone on the secretary's desk rang.

"Look," said Charles abruptly, "I'm going to the pub opposite. The Green Man. If you fancied a drink after your interview . . ."

"Oh . . . er . . . well . . ." She looked confused, like a small child, in spite of her adult clothes. She was dressed in the style of that summer, a sort of punk-with-the-rough-edges-smoothed-off, skin-tight black and white striped trousers and a fluorescent purple shirt with a black snake-skin tie.

"Dana will see you now, Miss Rawsleigh," said the secretary in a voice which disapproved of middle-aged men trying to pick up nubile teenagers.

"Yes. Well, er, fine . . . Yes, well, I might see you . . ." And Henry bobbed off into Dana's office.

Charles caught the secretary's eye and felt stupid. For once he hadn't been making an advance. He just wanted to talk to anyone who had a connection, however distant, with events at Tryst on the Saturday night.

He was drawing to the end of his second pint and thinking it was about time he got back to Hereford Road when, to his surprise, Henry appeared. She gave him a slightly self-conscious little wave, and then went across to a table where another girl was sitting. The two immediately broke into animated conversation.

Oh dear, thought Charles, this really is embarrassing. I just mention meeting in the pub and she's already fixed to see her friend here. Cue for Paris to down remainder of pint and make hasty getaway.

But before he could complete this plan of action the two girls were standing in front of him.

"Mr Paris," said Henry with great politeness, "could I introduce my sister Honoria. Hobby, this is Charles Paris."

"How do you do?"

The second girl gave him a firm handshake. She was probably some five years older than her sister, and in the distribution of family looks she had been the loser. The hair, blond in Henry, was a duller mouse colour in Hobby. The eyes, still blue, were smaller, and set either side of a determinedly large nose. Henry's ample curves contrasted with Hobby's almost boylike flatness.

But she was not unattractive. There was life and humour in the face as she said to Charles, "I gather you've just been to see Dana Wilson too."

"Yes. I'm afraid I don't think mine was a very profitable interview. What about yours, Henry?"

The girl's brow wrinkled childishly. "Well, I don't *know*. I mean, perhaps I didn't know what to expect—I haven't done many of those sort of interviews—but I'm afraid I just couldn't work out what she was talking about."

"Not much, if she said the same to you as she did to me."

"No. I mean, a friend gave me the introduction to her . . ."

Probably without her blush Charles could have made the connection, through *Lexton and Sons*, of Dana Wilson and Bertram Pride.

"And he didn't really tell me what it'd be like, but I suppose I vaguely thought she'd talk about, you know, prospects for work and what sort of stuff I'd done, but all she did seem to talk about was all the things she'd done in the past."

"You did have exactly the same interview as me."

"It was very strange."

"It's a very strange business you've got yourself into," said Hobby, in a tone of humorous reproach.

"I gather you're not in the theatre."

"God, no." The elder girl shuddered at the thought. "No, I have a nice, respectable, sensible job as a secretary at Conservative Central Office. Henry's the stage-struck idiot in our family." But it was not said without affection.

"Actually . . ." Henry giggled, "I'm quite glad that Dana didn't ask me what work I'd done, because I'm afraid there isn't that much to tell."

"We all had to start somewhere," Charles comforted.

"Yes, but really mine's all just school and, you know, college. Hardly, you know, much to write home about."

"Not that Daddy'd be very interested if you did."

"Your father doesn't approve of the theatre?"

"Well, I don't think he minds the theatre *as such*." Henry's brow wrinkled again. "But Daddy's a businessman, and I don't think he thinks the theatre is a very good *investment*."

"He is one hundred per cent right. Anyone who's looking for an investment shouldn't touch the theatre with a barge-pole."

"Anyway," Henry continued, "I suppose he is being quite decent about it. He says he'll support me for a year while I try to get started, and if I'm not on my own two feet by the end of that, then he wants me to do something else."

"So I think you'd better start thinking about what you're going to do next year," Hobby remarked rather tartly.

"Don't you be a pig!" Henry was instantly back to the nursery. "I am jolly well going to make a go of it, just you wait and see."

Charles intervened before Hobby could come back with a riposte. "I'm sure you will, Henry. If you work at it, and if you're really determined, you'll get there."

He wasn't sure to what extent he believed these platitudes, but they were obviously the right things to say to Henry, who positively glowed as she heard them.

"Yes, that's what I think. I'm sure it's just a matter of making the right contacts. I've heard it said that in the theatre it's not *what* you know, it's *who* you know." This was pronounced with great gravity, as if it was an observation of profound originality.

"I'm sure that's true," Charles agreed, equally gravely.

"But the trouble is, I don't really know many people 'in the business'." The phrase was put into quotation marks with some daring. "I mean, I've got lots of friends, you know, from home and school, but they're mostly doing dreary things like Cordon Bleu courses and they don't seem to know the right sort of people. Not for the theatre. Not the sort of people who are going to be of help to me.

And Daddy's friends are all useless—they're sort of Chairmen of ICI and frightfully draggy things like that."

She must have misinterpreted Charles's expression, because she added hastily, "You mustn't think I just want to get into the theatre through other people. I really am prepared to work hard . . . I mean, all the hours there are. Really. And I do go and work out at the Dance Centre and that sort of thing. It's just I'm sure I do need to meet people 'in the business'."

"Hence," said Hobby, again with some asperity, "the attraction of Bertram Pride."

Predictably this produced a blush from her younger sister, as Hobby went on, "Have you heard about this bit of cradle-snatching, Charles?"

"Well, yes," he replied awkwardly. "I did in fact meet Henry with Bertram last Saturday."

"Of course. Just before they went off for their dirty weekend."

"Hobby, it wasn't like that."

"What, the gossip columnists got it wrong?"

"No, it's . . . just . . ." Henry looked even more confused.

"According to the *Mail*, Bertram took you to Tryst and then spirited you away to his Bluebeard's Castle in Kent."

"I know you don't approve of my seeing Bertram."

"It's up to you who you do rude things with, Henry. I just think it would have been more sensible to choose someone nearer your own age than Daddy's."

"I'm old enough to choose for myself who I go out with."

"Of course, dear. Eighteen. A great age. I just can't imagine that a certain person from Gloucestershire can be too happy about the Bertram Pride connection."

"You mean your father wouldn't approve?" Charles elbowed his way back into the conversation.

"I can't think Daddy'd be over the moon about it. But he wasn't the person I was referring to," said Hobby with a hard look at her sister.

Henry looked close to tears; clearly she was finding the emotional strain of her affair with an older man hard to cope with. Charles came to the rescue with a blatant change of subject.

"Erm . . . any other interviews or auditions on the horizon, Henry?"

Hobby gave him an ironical look, well aware of what he was doing, but was content to withdraw from the sisterly bickering.

"Not a huge amount, no." Henry was relieved by the change of direction. "In fact, nothing, really. There's an agent I got an introduction to from . . . someone, but he's away on holiday at the moment."

Not Maurice Skellern, surely, thought Charles. He wouldn't wish that fate on any young aspirant in the theatre.

But Henry quickly defused that idea. "Chap called Freddie Winston . . . don't know if you've heard of him . . . ?"

Bertram Pride's agent, as it happened. "Oh yes. He's quite big in the business. Lot of famous clients."

"Yes. Don't know what chance there is of his taking one on . . ."

Absolutely none, if one were making the approach as just any would-be actress without an Equity card. As Bertram Pride's bit of stuff, though, one might meet a different reaction.

"Otherwise, not a lot happening?"

"No, actually the scene's a bit draggy at the moment. Lots of people away, no one seems to be casting much . . ."

"You don't have to tell me."

Hobby, who felt she had been silent too long, snorted. "Can't understand why you voluntarily go through all this agony. You ought to both get nice jobs in the Civil Service."

"Don't be silly, Hobby. As you say, you just don't understand." Henry turned her back dramatically on her sister and faced Charles. He suddenly realized his attraction for her. He was "someone in the business", perhaps a potential interpreter of the vagaries of the theatrical profession.

"I did see one thing coming up," Henry continued, looking closely at him with disconcerting earnestness. "It was advertised in *Stage*. A general audition for a musical."

"Oh yes." Charles spoke without enthusiasm.

"I mean, do you think it'd be worth one going along?"

He grimaced. The straight answer was of course that there was absolutely no point in someone of her limited experience and lack of union card going within a million miles of that sort of audition, but he didn't want to depress her too much.

"Well, Henry, there are always hundreds, thousands even, who do go along, and they tend to be pretty grim occasions . . ."

"Yes, I'm sure. I'm not thinking one might get a part or anything like that, I just think it could be frightfully good experience—the sort of thing one ought to *have done*."

"That is a point of view, yes."

"The audition's next Wednesday morning at the King's Theatre."

"Oh yes."

"The trouble is . . ." Henry paused. "I am frightfully weedy about that sort of thing. You know, not knowing exactly where to go, what to do . . ."

"There's not much to it."

"No, but I'd feel so much happier going along with someone who knew the ropes, someone who'd done that sort of thing before . . ."

"Oh yes." Charles looked up, suddenly aware of the direction her speech was taking. The appeal in the huge blue eyes would have melted the Colossus of Rhodes. "You mean you'd like me to go along to this audition with you?"

"Oh, Charles!" She clapped her hands delightedly. "I'd be frightfully chuffed if you would."

That evening Charles sat in his bedsitter, trying to read and trying to pretend he'd never thought of the idea of going to the pub or the Montrose. Two evenings in the latter with Zoë had made quite a hole in the old finances and if he was reduced to living on just what he got from the Unemployment Office, a bit of serious back-pedalling was called for.

He ignored the house-bell when it rang, assuming that the visitor must be for one of the Swedish girls. A series of thin Swedish youths with spots and glasses appeared fairly regularly for the various wenches. Or perhaps it was always the same youth, who was working quietly through the occupants of the other bedsitters. Charles couldn't tell, but, if it was, he didn't envy the young man his task.

The bell went on ringing. All the Swedish girls must be out, probably with their Swedish youths or youth, engaged in some

Swedish recreation. Charles went downstairs and opened the front door.

Kevin O'Rourke was standing there. Charles realized with a shock that this was the first time he had ever seen the man without his partner. O'Rourke without Bartlemas was an incomplete and disturbing sight.

Charles could not suppress the instinctive question. "Where's Bartlemas? Is he all right?"

"Yes, he's gone to a first night at Wyndhams."

"And you haven't gone with him?"

"No. I'm afraid I'm in no state for the theatre. May I come in?"

"Of course."

Few visitors ever came to Charles's bedsitter, but Kevin O'Rourke did not pass comment on the dusty piles of books and unmade bed. He was too upset for his customary fastidiousness to assert itself.

Before Charles had time to offer coffee (without milk—he never seemed to get round to buying any) or the scant remains of his last emergency half-bottle of Bell's, O'Rourke said, "I've heard more from the police."

"About Tristram? Have they found his—" Charles stopped himself just in time from saying "body", and finished lamely, "him?"

"No. But they've checked his movements as far as they can on the night Yves was killed. He certainly caught the six-thirty ferry on the Sunday morning, because one of the officials remembered him being very flustered and saying he'd had to change his plans and his friend couldn't come. Then he must have driven fairly flat out for the house at Mas-de-Pouzard, because a local farmer saw the Volvo parked outside early on the Monday morning."

"In other words he followed exactly the plan that he and Yves had made. Except he was on his own and Yves . . ."

O'Rourke winced.

Charles shook his head slowly. "So I suppose the police view of suicide is the most likely explanation. If he was going to do a bunk, why did he leave the car at the house? Why not drive on further or hide himself somewhere totally different? The police were bound to look at Mas-de-Pouzard, weren't they?"

"On the other hand . . ." O'Rourke's voice was hard. On his own he seemed much more serious and positive than he did in the company of Bartlemas. "If he was planning to commit suicide, why did he bother to go all that way? He could kill himself anywhere. Why didn't he do it in the flat?"

"I don't know. But he must have been in shock. I mean . . . after what happened. And I think it's quite common for people in shock just to get on with whatever they were doing, follow arrangements that they've made. It gives them something to do, shuts off what's happened from their minds. So I suppose, after he'd killed Yves, he just went through the motions of driving down to France, as they'd arranged . . . and it was only when he got to the house, when he actually stopped, that the full horror hit him and . . ."

"That's your solution, is it?" asked O'Rourke as Charles tailed off.

"Well, what other solution could there be?" Charles shrugged. "All right, he might still be alive. We mustn't assume suicide . . . at least until his body's found. But it does seem likely. Tristram was a pretty emotional guy. He's not the sort to take committing a murder in his stride."

In the silence that followed O'Rourke shook his head wearily. "So you're convinced that Tristram killed Yves?"

Charles gazed at his visitor in amazement. "Well, yes. I mean, that does seem to be the one certainty in this case. We and a whole restaurantful of people saw Tristram threaten Yves with a knife, we know that he was unhappy about Yves's promiscuity . . . And then the way the murder was done . . . I mean, with Yves naked . . . and the way he had been slashed around the genitals . . . There was no reason for that, not to kill him. That must have been sexual jealousy." Charles paused. "I'm sorry, O'Rourke. I know he was your cousin and you're fond of him, but I really don't think there is any other way of looking at the case."

The next words were spoken with slow intensity. "Charles, I want you to think of other ways of looking at it."

"What do you mean?"

"Ten years ago you found out how Marius Steen died. I want you to do the same now with Yves Lafeu."

"But, O'Rourke, in the case of Marius Steen, there was at least a mystery. Here, to think of any solution other than the obvious one involves incredible mental contortions."

"I want you to go through those mental contortions, Charles."

"But—"

"Please. Just think about it, just bring your mind to bear on it. Look, I know I'm being illogical, but I just cannot believe that Tristram would have killed Yves. He would be annoyed with him, furious with him, but he just wouldn't have done that. I'm sure."

"Hmm. What's your alternative explanation?"

"I don't know. That's why I've come to you. You're good at this sort of thing."

"Not very, I'm afraid."

"Oh, please, Charles. Just think it through with me."

"Sure, I'll do that, but I don't think we'll get far."

"I'll pay you. For your time. For your services."

Charles shook his head wryly. "I'm not a detective, O'Rourke. I'm an actor. Still, I'll play along. Let's have a drink."

He shared out the remains of his emergency Bell's into two glasses, one slightly chipped, which had been given away with soap powder.

"Right, let's start from the premise that Tristram didn't murder Yves, unlikely though it is. Under those circumstances, who did? Do you have any suspicions?"

O'Rourke shook his balding head dolefully.

"Well, Zoë certainly hated them both. She's in a pretty strange emotional state, so I suppose she might have done something stupid. Who else is there? Monique, Yves's sister. Don't know anything about her, but maybe she nursed some grudge from childhood against her brother. Jealous of his beauty, perhaps. Or what about the blond boy, the one who came to the restaurant and caused all the fuss? Perhaps he had some reason to hate Yves or . . . I'm sorry, O'Rourke, I'm really clutching at straws. And I don't think I'm getting anywhere. I mean, just thinking of that boy . . . Gary . . . brings it all back. We saw it. He was the cause of their quarrel. His arrival set the whole thing in motion, didn't it?"

"Yes. Very neatly. Rather too neatly, to my mind."

"What do you mean by that?"

"I've been thinking about it. Why did the boy, Gary, arrive at that moment?"

"He said he'd come to meet someone."

"Yes, but it was after eleven o'clock. The restaurant wouldn't have taken a booking for that time. Yves was already doing his lap of honour."

"Which was why he saw the boy."

"Yes, half an hour earlier and they wouldn't have met."

"That's true."

"And I thought the boy looked genuinely surprised to see Yves. The chances are that if they'd met through the Sparta or somewhere like that, the previous encounter would have been purely physical. Yves certainly wouldn't have talked about what he did for a living. Probably wouldn't even have used his real name."

"Hmm."

"And Yves also seemed to be surprised. He said the boy hadn't come by arrangement."

"Yes, he said, but—"

"All right. He may have been lying. He was certainly quite capable of it. But there was something odd about it. The boy said he had a date to meet a Mr Carruthers. Well, there certainly wasn't anyone sitting alone at a table, waiting. Everyone was in couples, or parties."

"Maybe he lied."

"Yes. Just seems a very specific lie. Why 'Mr Carruthers'? Is that the sort of name you think up on the spur of the moment?"

"It could be."

"All right. But there was another thing that was odd."

"What?"

"Monique was on the door to check the reservations, take coats, give them back to people as they left, and so on . . ."

"Yes."

"Well, she knew how the restaurant worked. She knew when last orders were. Why did she let Gary in? Why didn't she just tell him that Tryst was closed and he must have got the wrong end of the stick about there being a reservation?"

Charles was silent, as he ran the scene through his mind. Yes, now

76

O'Rourke mentioned it, the sequence of events had been odd. "What do you want me to do?"

"I want you to talk to Monique. And I want you to track down that boy Gary."

Charles grunted a laugh. "Just that?"

"For the moment, yes. Will you? Please."

He agreed. Just as he had agreed to accompany Henry to the general audition. Dear oh dear, he thought, I'm becoming a soft touch.

Chapter Seven

TALKING TO MONIQUE and tracking down Gary proved not to be easy. Charles had airily agreed to help O'Rourke without actually thinking how he was going to make contact with either of them, and when he did think about the problem, on the Saturday morning, he realized that he had no idea of what his approach should be.

Except for the fact that the girl was called Monique Lafeu, he knew nothing about her. The only people he knew who might be able to give him an address, her brother and Tristram Gowers, were unavailable to be asked. O'Rourke, whom he rang, didn't have any ideas. Charles had hoped O'Rourke might know some of the other waiters or staff at Tryst, but this was not the case. He and Bartlemas, like Charles, had known only the proprietor and chef.

Charles tried ringing Zoë, but was quite relieved that she was out. He didn't think she'd be very pleased to be asked about the sister of Yves Lafeu. Nor did he think it likely that she would know where the girl lived.

Of course it was quite possible that Monique was not in the country. Tryst, after all, was to have been closed completely for four weeks, so it was likely that all of the staff would be taking their holidays at the same time. Monique might well have returned to family or friends in France. But if that had happened, she would probably have been summoned back by the police after her brother's murder . . .

Charles had to admit he just did not know. And he couldn't think of any way of finding out. He tried looking up "Lafeu, Monique" in the telephone directory, but was unsurprised to find no such entry. Not for the first time in his dabblings in investigation, he felt envious of the police's resources in research and information. The odds, he reflected, are very much stacked against the amateur detective.

The phone-book was no more helpful in his search for Gary Stane. He hadn't really thought it would be; an entry in the directory implies a permanence of address which did not match the boy's manner and appearance. Charles could remember Gary's camp theatricality well, and was sure he would recognize the boy again. The question was, where to start looking.

Of course, Tristram had referred to Gary as Yves's "bit of Sparta rough trade", so perhaps investigation should start at the Sparta Club, wherever that might be.

It was not a lead Charles relished following up. He was not prejudiced against gays; he had worked in the theatre so long that he no longer particularly noticed people's sexual proclivities; but he felt a kind of social unease about the prospect of entering a gay club. He was not worried about being seen there or being the subject of unwelcome advances; he just didn't feel confident about doing the right things at the right time, like an Anglican going to a Catholic Mass. But he realized he might have to overcome his shyness and make the attempt.

Before he did that, he thought of another approach. Gary, he remembered, on arriving at Tryst, had said he was expecting to meet "*a* Mr Carruthers". The use of the article suggested that he had yet to meet the Mr Carruthers in question. He had also said, "It's been arranged."

The two facts could be interpreted, as O'Rourke had suggested, to mean that the boy's appearance had been set up, deliberately stage-managed to precipitate a public row between Tristram and Yves, and provide an apparent motive for the murder to come.

If that had been the case, what would be the simplest way of arranging it? And what sort of person finds nothing unusual in the idea of turning up at a restaurant to meet an unknown man?

It didn't take Charles long to think of an escort agency. A few actors and actresses of his acquaintance eked out their incomes during lean patches by doing escort work (and had provided him with some hilarious and pathetic stories from their experiences). His friends had worked for heterosexual agencies, but he felt sure that there were parallel set-ups for gays.

He decided he needed to do a bit of background reading.

Westbourne Grove is a good place for shopping if you're interested in either overpriced one-bedroom flats, cheap air-tickets, Islam or sex.

For the last-named there are a few specialist shops, but all the newsagents carry a large and varied stock of hardish pornography and contact magazines. Charles had never taken much notice of this display in the papershop where he bought his *Times* every morning, and was surprised at the range of material available. Since most of the magazines were sealed in transparent plastic, he found it difficult to make his selection. He knew that what he wanted was homosexual, but he did not want to end up with an album of posing boys. After all, an agency whose clients booked into Tryst was not down the meat-rack end of the market; it would be likely to advertise in a journal bought by the more sophisticated and discriminating gay.

"Can I help you, sir?" asked the impassive Pakistani from whom he bought his paper every morning.

"Yes. Thank you. I'll have a *Times*, please, and . . . er . . . I wanted a magazine . . ."

"Yes, sir. What magazine?"

"A sort of . . . specialist magazine."

"Computing, is it you want? Video games? Hang-gliding?"

"Er, no. It's . . . um . . . I want a magazine which has advertisements in it for gay escort agencies."

"Certainly, sir." The shopkeeper reached across into the rack and instantly picked out a yellow-covered publication called *Patroclus*. He certainly knew his stock. "This is what you want, sir."

As Charles reached into his pocket for the rather large amount of money that was required, he heard a disgusted snort behind him.

One of the Swedish girls from the Hereford Road house was staring at him with frosty Scandinavian disapproval.

Patroclus was quite a revelation for Charles. He did not find anything to shock him in it, but he was surprised by what a well-organized and detailed culture the magazine revealed. No doubt he would have had the same reaction had he bought the publications on computers, video games or hang-gliding which the newsagent had recommended.

Still, in the back pages he found the information he required. A large number of escort agencies offered discreet and efficient service. In fact, he was daunted by the number of them. Presumably they represented only a fraction of those that existed in the capital. The odds against tracking down Gary Stane by that method lengthened.

Still, his only other lead was the Sparta Club. It was worth trying a few agencies first.

For no very good reason he felt coy about using his own voice for his enquiries. He wondered what identity he should use instead. For an actor the voice is everything. Who should he be?

He had played his share of mincing queens in his time. He'd done Gorringe in Peter Shaffer's *Black Comedy* at Birmingham ("I have always thought this play was actor-proof; last night's cast proved me wrong"—*Birmingham Post*). Then he'd appeared in the very, very short run of a play set backstage at a drag beauty contest ("I should think Gay Lib will ask the author of this awful little piece to go back in again"—*The Listener*). But he didn't think either voice was right for the task in hand. The sort of people who used the services of gay escort agencies would, he felt sure, not be flamboyant effeminates but serious businessmen down in London for a meeting or conference.

That gave him a bit of a lead. He tried to think of the characters of that sort that he had played. There had been a carpet salesman in a rather awful thriller at Worthing ("Charles Paris seemed to be acting in a different play from the rest of the cast—and who could blame him?"—*Worthing Gazette*). That had been a sort of indeterminate Midlands accent. Then he'd used Bristolian as a purser in an episode of an interminable series about a cruise liner ("What Charles Paris was doing in the cast I could not fathom"—*Sunday Telegraph*). Trouble was . . . Bristolian always sounded slightly funny, as if the speaker was sending himself up.

Yes. He got it. The South London twang he had used as an insurance assessor in another thriller, *Dead To The World*, at Worthing ("I have been more thrilled by a cup of cold tea"—*Worthing Gazette*).

He dialled the first number on the page.

"Hello, One-Off Escort Services."

It was a girl's voice. He was relieved to find someone there on a Saturday, though when he thought about it, that was only logical. The weekend must be the busiest time for that sort of service, as the lonely desperately try to avoid spending Saturday night alone in the city.

"Er, yes. Good morning. I am, er, down in London on business." It struck Charles that he should have used a more provincial accent. His voice placed him somewhere in mid-Croydon, which hardly justified staying in town after meetings. Never mind, he couldn't change accent now. And no doubt the girl at the other end of the phone had heard a good few lies in the course of her work. He pressed on. "Yes, and I, er, seem to find myself at a loose end this evening, and thought it would be rather nice to, er, have some . . ."

"Company?"

"Yes. Exactly." Then, following the instincts of Charles Paris rather than those of the character he was playing, he hastened to add, "I mean, just for a drink, or dinner or . . . I wasn't thinking of anything more, er, you know . . ."

"Just as well," the girl said frostily. "Ours is purely a service to provide escorts. We are not a sexual contact agency."

"No, no, of course not."

"That would be illegal," she averred primly.

"Yes, yes, I understand that."

He was trying to sound properly chastened, but she obviously took his tone for disappointment. "On the other hand . . ." she began more cheerily, "we have effected introductions which have led to . . . more romantic associations. It often happens that good friendships are formed through meetings we arrange. And, of course," she concluded, removing any vestigial ambiguity from her speech, "what our escorts do in their own time is their own business. But for the fee you pay us all you are buying is a pleasant companion for the evening."

Charles got the picture. "Yes, well, as I say, it is, er, company that I'm after."

"Well, we have a very charming selection of young men on our books. I take it you would like someone in the younger age-bracket?"

"Oh yes. I think I would like a young man. In his twenties, say . . . And tall and blond."

"I'm sure we'll be able to accommodate you, Mr Smith."

"I didn't say my name was Smith."

"Oh, didn't you?" Charles could feel her stopping herself from saying, "Everyone else does." Instead, she just apologized.

"I'm really looking for a boy called Gary," said Charles.

"Ah, well, I'm sure one of our escorts wouldn't mind being called Gary if that's what you want."

"No. I mean a specific boy called Gary. I'm trying to make contact with a young man called Gary Stane."

"We have no escort of that name on our books." The voice was all frosty again.

"But I'm just trying to find this boy . . . tallish, as I say, blond . . . good-looking . . ."

"We have plenty of other escorts quite as good-looking."

"It's not just looks I'm after. I just want this one boy."

"I'm afraid we're not a Missing Persons Bureau."

With that the girl rang off. Charles sighed and replaced the receiver on the payphone.

"You are an old filthy perversion."

He turned round, to find himself staring into the baleful eyes of the Swede from the newsagents. He didn't know how long she had been standing on the landing listening.

He tried ringing a few more agencies, but with diminishing confidence. The services that they offered were disguised in phrases of varying subtlety, but none of them had heard of Gary Stane. And all of them clammed up when they realized that he was searching for one specific person rather than a nameless stranger. Charles decided that he could spend months ringing round all the available agencies, and still have no certainty of finding his quarry.

So that left the Sparta Club . . .

Patroclus provided the address in its comprehensive clubs listings. Charles had been expecting somewhere in Soho and was surprised to find that the club was in Leominster Terrace, in that hinterland of hotels, flat conversions and private clinics between Queensway and Paddington.

Nor did he find the club's frontage as he had expected it when he presented himself there at half-past nine that Saturday evening. His mental projection had been of something Soho and shoddy, with garish neons and thumping music like a strip club. He had not been prepared for the white portico and huge black door, nor the discreet brass plate beside it, reading "Sparta Club—Members Only". The impression was of the embassy of a small but prosperous foreign power.

Charles had delayed his visit till half-past nine for a very simple reason, which he was almost ashamed to admit to himself. It was just that he knew it would be dark by then, and though he was not a man who had any reputation or image to lose, he still felt a degree of embarrassment about his mission.

The man behind the table in the entrance hall had the air of the *maître d'hôtel* in an expensive restaurant and his first appraising look made Charles feel perhaps he should have excavated his one suit from his wardrobe for the occasion.

"Good evening, sir. Can I help you?"

Two middle-aged men and a young one, all dressed in suits, entered from the street. While the young man was being signed into the visitors' book, Charles had a moment to decide his approach.

But the diversion didn't last long. Again Charles found himself looking into the sceptical eyes of the man behind the desk.

"Yes?"

Oh well, direct approach was as good as any.

"Er, good evening." He had been intending to stick with the Croydon insurance assessor persona, but found himself instinctively upgrading his accent to the one he had used as Major Petkoff in *Arms And The Man* ("Surely crustier than Shaw intended" – *Western Evening Record*). "I'm trying to make contact with a young man called Gary Stane."

"Really, sir? May I ask if you're a member of the Sparta Club?"

"No, I'm not."

"Then I'm afraid I can't help you." The man turned back to some bills he was studying on the desk.

"But all I want is an address or telephone number for him."

The man looked up again, scepticism giving way now to anger. "I'm sure that's all you want, sir. That's all a lot of people want. To

84

invade privacy. And our club is set up to guard the privacy of its members."

"But I . . . Can't you even tell me if Gary Stane is a member?"

"No."

"I suppose I couldn't join?" asked Charles in some desperation.

"I think you could safely suppose that. Unless, of course, you could find two members to propose and second you. Then your name would in due course be put up to the selection committee."

"And what is the membership fee?"

The man told him. Charles reeled out in shock. He felt as if he'd just been blackballed for the Garrick Club.

He rang O'Rourke mid-morning on the Sunday to report progress. Since he had made none, that didn't take long. O'Rourke had managed to contact one of Tryst's waiters, but got no lead on finding Monique Lafeu. However, the older man seemed anxious to talk further about the murder and invited Charles out to Islington for lunch. The actor had, as usual, not made any other plans, so he accepted the offer gratefully.

Sundays he'd never really sorted out. Throughout his childhood they had been days of ritual tedium, punctuated rather than enlivened by church, days when sneaking upstairs to do homework had been a welcome alternative to genteel conversation and helping in the garden. Anything was better than that kind of regime, so he had quite welcomed National Service, when duties did not often coincide with the normal working week and Sunday was just another in an interminable sweep of indistinguishable days, church parades seeming to Charles not that different from any other sort of parade. Then had come Oxford, when Sundays suddenly came into their own. With guaranteed freedom from lectures and tutorials, without even the tiny feeling of guilt that the Bodleian was open, Charles and his friends had lazed and chatted. It was during that period that he had first begun to concentrate on what was to be a lifetime hobby for him—drinking. At the same time his interest in the theatre was developing and Sunday afternoons would often be amiably mopped up by rehearsal for OUDS or college productions.

And when he started working in the professional theatre Sundays again conveniently merged, camouflaged, into the rest of the calendar. In weekly rep., of which he had a few years, Sunday was the busiest day of the week. They would start to clear the previous week's set as soon as the curtain went down on the Saturday night, and then, often working through, erect the new one. In those days the demarcations between actors and backstage staff had been less rigidly defined, with the result that everyone did a bit of everything. Sundays were days of convivial panic, one minute supporting a flat, the next painting it, knocking props together, mending fuses in the lighting-box, donning unfamiliar costumes and negotiating unfamiliar sets in hysterically unprepared dress-rehearsals, trying every minute to cram the words of the new play into a mind which hadn't quite flushed out the lines of the last, and all working towards what most of the time seemed to be the impossible aim of opening the show before a paying audience on the Monday night.

But all that had changed. Now, on the occasions when he was in work, Charles hardly ever worked on a Sunday. Equity, ever protective of its members' interests, had finally managed to impose some regulation on the number of hours that could be demanded of actors, and brought such modern concepts as overtime into a business where for so long the work ethics of nineteenth-century cotton-mills had operated. The result had been a change in the pattern of production in repertory theatres. Weekly rep. had given way to fortnightly; and then three-weekly, or even longer, intervals between new productions became the norm. And the costs of overtime meant that most actors got their Sundays off, and the new shows would most likely open on Wednesdays rather than Mondays.

Charles knew the changes were a Good Thing, a very belated improvement in working conditions. But he couldn't help feeling a bit of nostalgia for the old days. In weekly rep. there had never been time for anything except doing the current show and getting the next one on. He knew he had been less depressed in those days than he had since; there just hadn't been the time.

And in the midst of that manic activity, when he wasn't working, when he had the odd day off, there had been little oases of married Sundays with Frances. Before Juliet, their daughter, was born, these had been days of Sunday papers and sex, late rising and pub, with

86

often an afternoon return to bed for more Sunday papers and sex. With the advent of Juliet, and the purchase of the Muswell Hill house, this occasional pattern had changed. Less time for the Sunday papers and the sex (though neither was ignored completely), more "doing things in the house", "pottering in the garden" and eating too much of traditional roasts and two vegetables. Their Sundays together had become, in fact, a parody of the childhood Sundays Charles had spent with his parents. The difference was that he enjoyed the times with Frances and Juliet. He was away a lot, working, and so those days retained their rarity value. He had no opportunity to get bored with them, and even felt the actor's satisfaction from having given a good performance in his role as conventional husband, father and rate-payer.

But then he and Frances had drifted apart . . .

He realized on that Sunday morning that he should ring her. Thinking back made him nostalgic for her. He even had a flash of his much-discredited fantasy that they might get back together again. Sometimes, just intellectually, it could seem so simple. But he knew that all of their attempts to live together again had failed, not in scenes of violence and anger, just in the rueful recognition that neither of them had changed and that the differences in their priorities which had led Charles to leave Frances in 1961 remained, more than twenty years later, a continuing source of mutual exasperation. The affection survived, but their ability to cohabit decreased with each passing year.

And now of course there was David. Now Frances was talking of a divorce. Now she was going to start a new life with her schools inspector.

Or probably was.

Charles couldn't summon up the nerve to ring her for a precise definition of her plans. At least ignorance left the possibility of hope.

"And are you two actually members of the Sparta Club?"

O'Rourke shook his head. The strands of hair, apparently glued across its baldness, did not stir. "No, not quite our scene. We've got a lot of chums who are members, though."

"Perhaps some of them might have a lead on Gary Stane?"

"Possibly. Certainly worth asking. Though I doubt if we'll get anywhere."

"Why not?"

"Well, you see, I'm sure that a boy like Gary Stane wouldn't actually be a *member*. Too young, for one thing. And I wouldn't have thought he could afford the membership."

"No," said Charles, remembering the figure he had been quoted.

"So it's most likely that he'd gone along as someone's guest."

"And met Yves?"

"Yes. And they'd got on together . . . or got off together, if you prefer, but it's quite possible that that was the only occasion when Gary went to the club."

"Hmm. Anyway, if you could ask . . ."

"I will."

"And I'll try to think of some other approach."

Charles sipped at his glass of icy *kir*. O'Rourke seemed more relaxed than he had on the Friday evening. At that time the surprise of seeing him without Bartlemas had made Charles fear that there might be some rift in the relationship, but that was obviously not the case. William Bartlemas, realizing how deeply O'Rourke was taking Yves's death and the suspicions of Tristram, though unable himself to take them so to heart, was showing great care and solicitude for his friend. He was in the kitchen, discreetly preparing lunch, leaving O'Rourke and Charles the opportunity to talk.

"I suppose," Charles asked diffidently, "you haven't had any other thoughts as to who might have killed Yves? As always, assuming it wasn't Tristram."

O'Rourke shook his head again. "Sorry."

"We talked a bit about motive, and we only came up with Zoë, who certainly hated them both, and Monique, for reasons we cannot begin to imagine, and Gary Stane . . . I don't know, because of some sort of sexual jealousy?"

"It's not a lot, is it?"

"No, but suppose we approach it from the other end—opportunity."

"What, you mean who could have got into the flat and killed Yves?"

"Not just that. I mean, if you are thinking of a planned murder,

88

then you have to think of a murderer who knew Tristram and Yves well enough to have heard the details of their holiday plans."

"Why?"

"The choice of that night to kill Yves wouldn't have been random. I was talking this through with Stan Fogden, you know, the bloke who was with me when we found the body. Now if the murderer did know about the holiday, but didn't know that Tristram had arranged to have the flat decorated, then he might safely assume that Yves's body would not be found for a full month."

"Yes, I see what you mean." O'Rourke looked excited; then saw a snag. "What about Tristram?"

"Well, this bit is pure conjecture, but let's just imagine for a moment that our murderer breaks into the flat—no, no signs of forcible entry—is *let* into the flat . . . which again suggests that he or she was known to Tristram and Yves . . . and draws a gun on them."

"But Yves was killed with a knife," O'Rourke objected.

"Wait till I've finished. He—or she—holds them both at gunpoint, gets Yves to strip naked and kills him with the knife, mutilating his body in a way that will suggest sexual jealousy and turn the suspicion on to Tristram . . ."

"And Tristram's watched all this?"

"Maybe. I don't know. Anyway, then the murderer turns his gun on Tristram and threatens to kill him too, unless he gets into the car and drives it, according to plan, down to France."

"But how does our murderer get on to the ferry? Or through passport control?"

"I don't know. Maybe he or she hides in the back of the Volvo, hidden under the luggage. Maybe goes on the ferry as a passenger. Let's not worry about the details for the moment. Okay, so the murderer gets Tristram to drive all the way down to Mas-de-Pouzard and then kills him. Kills him in a way that looks like suicide, and does it somewhere where the body is unlikely to be discovered for some time.

"So, so far as anyone in this country is concerned, Tristram and Yves are away for a month. No search-parties will be sent out till that month is over. I don't know what the house is like in France, how many friends they've got out there, but if the place is fairly remote, it's quite possible that none of the locals would be particularly interested in whether they were there or not.

"In that way, the murderer would have achieved a self-sealing crime. Yves's body is found at the end of September; then they start looking for Tristram's body—perhaps find it, perhaps don't—and the police think Tristram killed his lover in a mad fit of jealousy, drove off to France, thinking he might get away with it, realized the hopelessness of his position, and then killed himself."

"Which is exactly what they appear to think at the moment."

"Yes. A perfect crime, as far as someone who wanted to kill Tristram and Yves is concerned."

"Hmm." O'Rourke looked torn. He desperately wanted to believe any alternative to the idea of Tristram having killed Yves, but he was quite as aware as Charles of gaping holes and implausibilities in the storyline Charles had just outlined.

"I'm sorry, O'Rourke. But you did ask me to try and think of other ways of looking at the crime, and I've just produced one."

"Yes," O'Rourke said slowly. "And I'm very grateful to you. You never know, there might be something in it. But who? Who would do that?"

"Well, let's go back to the fact that there was no sign of a break-in. Tristram and Yves must have let in anyone who arrived to kill them."

"Unless the person was already there."

"You mean Monique?"

"Yes. Or someone who had been having dinner in the restaurant."

"What?" Charles laughed. "Sir John? Bernard Walton? Bertram Pride?"

"They all knew Tristram and Yves well."

"Yes, but what are we going to do—check through all the reservations for that evening and find out where all the people went when they left the restaurant? I think that might be difficult to do." He remembered something. "Though one, in fact, I've already done."

"Who?"

"Dear Bertram. Straight after he'd finished he spirited off his Rent-A-Tottie for a naughty weekend at his country cottage. I have that not only from the newspaper gossip columns, but from Rent-A-Tottie herself."

"You've met her since?"

"Yes. Sweet kid. Aspiring actress."

"What's she like?"

"Hmm. I think the word I would have to use is 'naive'."

The phone rang in another room. O'Rourke did not react, confident that Bartlemas would take it.

"In terms of thinking of our murderer, Charles, we must presumably pick on someone who wanted both Tristram and Yves out of the way."

"I don't know. If Tristram was a witness of the killing of Yves . . ."

"Someone capable of the kind of tortuous planning you've devised would surely have only done it that way to get rid of them both. If he just wanted Yves out of the way, there would have been much simpler ways of doing it."

"Yes, you're right. We need someone with a motive against both. I wonder if—"

He was interrupted by the appearance at the door of Bartlemas. His shirt-sleeves were rolled up and he was wearing his favourite apron, with an advertisement for "Camp Coffee" on it.

"O'Rourke, telephone for you . . ."

"What a time of day to call . . ."

"People just don't think, do they . . ."

"Just before Sunday lunch . . ."

"Meant to be a day of rest . . ."

"I don't know . . ."

Charles was amused to see how instantly O'Rourke dropped back into stereo conversation when his partner appeared.

O'Rourke rose from his chair. "Who is it then?"

"It's Monique Lafeu," said Bartlemas.

O'Rourke was gone some time. Bartlemas had apologized that he must "rush back to the kitchen and flagellate my mayonnaise", so Charles was left on his own.

The sitting-room, like the rest of the house, was filled with memorabilia of Kean and Macready. The dominant feature was a large gilt-framed painting over the fireplace. Experts at various museums and galleries had disputed the claim, but Bartlemas was in no doubt that the work was of Edmund Kean in one of his most famous parts, Sir Giles Overreach in *A New Way To Pay Old Debts*. It was very different from Clint's version in the Garrick Club, but the eyes were certainly demonic enough to justify the identification, and Charles always regarded the picture as a symbol of concentrated, but theatrical, evil.

The bookshelves contained a predictable collection. Barry Cornwall's *Life of Kean*, Lady Pollock's *Macready As I Knew Him*, Thomas Colley Grattan's *Beaten Paths And Those Who Trod Them*, Genest's *Account Of The English Stage*, and so on. But amongst the props of idol-worship were some more modern reference works. A complete set of *Who's Who In The Theatre*, going right back to the first edition of 1912. And the four volumes of the current *Spotlight*.

Spotlight is the producer's and casting director's bible, in which every actor and actress who can afford the fee (and a good few who can't) insert their photographs, agent's name and possibly details of recent work. The entries are telling. The height of panache is just to put in the name without a photograph, but that is a practice only indulged in by the hugest stars, totally confident of their universal recognition. The next step down is a half-page photograph in the "Leading" section; here extremely well-known faces mix with vaguely well-known faces and a few extremely optimistic faces. After comes "Character", a section into which some surprisingly famous actors and actresses put their half-page photographs, shrewdly aware that there are more character than leading parts around. Next comes "Younger Character", a section which, particularly in the "Actresses" volume, covers a remarkably wide age-range. (Actresses' photographs are also inclined to be a little misleading. It is usually safe to add ten years to what their *Spotlight* pictures look like.) Finally comes the "Young" section, though even that can provide a few surprises.

Charles could never see a set of *Spotlight* without reaching down the "Actors L-Z" volume and stealing a look at his entry. He knew it was pure self-indulgence, rather like an author looking himself up in a library catalogue, but it did give him reassurance that he existed. The fact that so many producers and casting directors must see his picture looking out at them as they flicked through the book made it only the more remarkable that his telephone rang so rarely.

Perhaps, he wondered as he looked at his photograph, it was a matter of expression. His face seemed to him to have a defeated air, like an unwanted puppy at Battersea Dogs' Home; it seemed to say to the prospective employer, "Oh, come on, I'm sure you can find someone better than *me*." Which, all too often, his prospective employers did.

"Maurice Skellern Artistes" didn't inspire confidence either. Once again Charles wondered whether he should try to join a better-known agency.

Nor did his list of credits change the image a lot. "RECENT TELEVISION: Barman in *The Strutters* (WET series)" was hardly going to send a Hollywood producer into paroxysms of enthusiasm.

Charles wondered if it would make any difference if next year he got himself categorized as "Leading" rather than "Character". Somehow he doubted it.

He was about to return the volume to the shelf when an idle thought struck him. Turning to the index at the front, he looked up under the "S"s.

And there it was. "STANE, Gary" and a page reference.

He was in the "Young" section, right at the back, where most of the hopefuls can only afford quarter-page pictures.

Though the hair was darker and longer, Charles recognized the pretty face with its defensive petulance.

"Maxine Ruttemann Agency", it said, with an address and phone-number.

At that moment O'Rourke came bubbling back into the room. "Monique," he announced, "she wants to meet and talk."

Things were beginning to move.

Chapter Eight

"MAXINE RUTTEMANN AGENCY," said a nasal female voice at the end of the telephone when Charles rang through on the Monday morning.

"Hello. I believe you have an actor called Gary Stane on your books."

"Yes."

"Oh, good. I'm trying to make contact with him."

"Is this theatrical work you're talking about?"

"Well . . ." An electric typewriter hummed over the line as Charles tried to frame his approach.

"I mean, is it an acting or a dancing job?" the girl's voice clarified.

"It isn't exactly a job," Charles confessed. "I just want to make contact with him."

"I see." The nasal voice took on a new scepticism. "I think perhaps you've come through to the wrong agency. I book Gary as an actor and dancer."

"Yes. But you must have a phone number for him. I'm sure you could—"

"His escort work," she continued, riding above his voice, "is handled by Intro/Outro."

She gave him the number and rang off abruptly.

Charles dialled the new number.

"Intro/Outro Agency." Again it was a female voice; again nasal; but this time it was American. Charles wondered. He was sure he could hear the same electric typewriter working away.

"Was I talking to you a moment ago?"

"Sorry?" asked the American voice.

"I was just talking to the Maxine Ruttemann Agency."

"This is the Intro/Outro Agency," the American voice repeated blandly. If she was the same girl, she certainly wasn't giving anything away.

"Yes. Of course. Listen, do you have a young man called Gary Stane on your books?"

"We have a lot of very charming escorts, sir, and I'm sure if you were looking for company, we could provide someone with whom you would have a most enjoyable evening."

"Yes. It's actually Gary Stane I want to meet."

"Have you spent an evening with him before?"

Her reply was incautious, implying that Gary Stane definitely was on the agency's books. Charles decided it was time for a little tactical lying. He wished he had started the conversation in his Croydon insurance assessor's voice, but pressed on in his own.

"Er, yes. Some months ago. Had a most pleasant time. And at the end of the evening I did say how . . . er, pleasant it would be if we could meet up again when I was next in London." There was a pause. The girl had not yet risen to the bait. "I come down on business from time to time," he went on.

"Yes." The girl spoke slowly, thinking. Her American accent sounded weaker. Charles was almost certain it was the girl from the Maxine Ruttemann Agency. "Well, listen, I think it might be possible to arrange another meeting with Gary."

"I would be most grateful."

"Presumably if you're only down on a brief trip, you'd like to meet soon."

"Please."

"This evening?"

"That would be ideal."

"Well, look, I'll have to speak to Gary and see if he's free. Is there a number where I can reach you?"

Charles felt disinclined to give the Hereford Road one. "Erm, no. I'm rather in transit at the moment. Between meetings. You know, I'm down for an insurance conference."

He tried to restrain the Croydon twang from creeping into his voice, but the image of the insurance assessor was becoming stronger by the minute. A hazard of acting is the tendency to build up a full background to every funny voice. Already Charles could visualize the young man with his guilty secret, the wife and two children secure on the Barratt estate in Milton Keynes, the occasional guilt-ridden indulgences (while on trips to London) in the "other side of his nature".

Mustn't let the fantasy get out of hand. "Perhaps I could ring you back in a couple of hours," he suggested, firmly sticking to his own voice.

"Yes, that'd be fine. Presumably," the American voice went on (she too seemed to have done a bit of mental sock-pulling-up and the accent was more assured), "since you've used the agency before, you know about our rates and arrangements."

"Remind me," said Charles, playing safe.

He reeled a bit at the figures mentioned. The investigation was going to prove rather expensive. Perhaps he should have taken up O'Rourke's offer of payment. Expenses, anyway. Yes, expenses. The word had a nice Philip Marlowe ring to it.

It occurred to him after he rang off that he needn't have followed this laborious and costly method of contacting Gary Stane. When he got through to the Maxine Ruttemann Agency, he could just have pretended to be a producer or casting director, said he had a part for which he thought Gary might be ideal, and fixed to meet and talk about it.

No actor would have refused that bait.

But, equally, no actor who had himself suffered the agony of disappointed hopes could stoop so low as to play that sort of trick on a fellow-member of his profession.

When he rang back an hour later, it was confirmed that Gary Stane would be free that evening. He would meet Charles for a pre-dinner drink in the bar of the St Nicholas Hotel near Oxford Circus. Charles was to tell the barman when he arrived, "just in case Gary didn't recognize him."

Charles felt extremely self-conscious sitting in the bar at eight o'clock that evening. The large Bell's in front of him was not having its customary calming effect. He had exhumed his one suit for the occasion, even brushed it, and its unaccustomed stiffness added to his unease. He had also gone to the lengths of digging out a tie, a paisley silk number whose colours had been rather subdued by removal with greasepainty fingers every night he wore it in *Rookery Nook* ("The production showed as much sense of humour as a cremation"—*Coventry Evening Telegraph*).

Charles felt ridiculously nervous. It wasn't like stage fright; with that, through all the anguish, you always have the confidence that the author's lines are there to fall back on (if you can remember them). It wasn't even like doing an impersonation, being in disguise as someone else, an exercise that Charles had undertaken a good few times in his career. No, on this occasion he had to be himself, and he had no idea how the evening would have to be played.

Gary Stane soon put him at his ease. Charles recognized the tall young man as he entered the characterless bar-room. The unlikely blondness of the hair stood out, and to make identification simpler, Gary was wearing exactly the same clothes as he had been on Charles's previous sighting of him. Maybe the blue and white striped shirt and the beige suit were his standard costume for dates. Maybe its colour or style had some particular significance to his usual hosts. Charles felt horribly out of his depth.

But Gary came across from the bar and gave him a firm handshake. "Mr Paris?"

"Oh, er, yes." Charles half-rose from his seat, then wondered whether that was the proper form for the circumstances. He sat back down again.

The young man sat opposite and looked at him expectantly. Gary was undoubtedly very beautiful. His skin was carefully tanned; the shirt was opened far enough down to show a long triangle of hairless brown chest. Only the unrealistic hair and a slight dullness in the blue eyes spoiled the image.

The silence had gone on some time before Charles realized his duty and waved for a waiter. "What will you have to drink, Gary?"

"Oh, a Campari soda would be very nice, Mr Paris." The boy smiled, revealing an orthodontist's dream of white teeth.

At least Charles felt financially secure for the evening. He had explained his problem to O'Rourke, who had instantly paid two hundred pounds into his account, so Charles had dared to draw out half of that. (Had he withdrawn a hundred without the subsidy, he would have worried about giving his bank manager a coronary.)

"It's very nice to see you again, Mr Paris," said Gary. He spoke with flat but punctilious elocution, like the Head Girl proposing a vote of thanks to the visiting speaker.

"You remember me?"

"Of course. How could I forget?"

This was said with an edge of automatic flirtatiousness. Just part of the job, Charles assumed. He felt certain Gary hadn't seen him at Tryst the night before Yves died, so the recognition must be pretended. Still, if the Intro/Outro Agency had reported his claim to have been out with Gary before, then Gary wasn't going to argue. If that was what the client wanted . . . It was quite possible that he spent so many such evenings, anyway, chatting away on automatic pilot, that he really didn't notice who he was with.

"Down in London on business, are you, Mr Paris?" Gary was doing his job well, not letting the pauses sag too long, keeping the conversation going. No doubt a lot of genuine lonely businessmen had been glad of his services.

"Yes, yes," said Charles. "Insurance conferences, meetings, that sort of thing."

"Must be interesting," Gary lied brightly.

Charles was having difficulty with his persona. As soon as he mentioned "insurance" the Croydon voice threatened. He really should have done a bit more preparation. He felt as if he were in the early days of rehearsal of a new play and he hadn't yet worked out which way to play his part.

"Yes, well, you know . . . Interesting some of the time. Every now and then. Most of the time dead boring. Like most jobs."

"Yes," Gary agreed, but without ironic comment on his own work. "That's why it's so nice to get out and have a fling, isn't it, Mr Paris?"

"Oh, yes."

"Actually . . ." Gary lowered his long eyelashes over his lifeless blue eyes, "I do feel a bit formal calling you Mr Paris. I'm sure you've got a Christian name . . . ?"

Charles found this flirtatiousness a little unnerving. "Charles. Er, Charles."

"Oh, that's a nice name."

Charles winced. The line was too mechanical. It reminded him uncomfortably of the few sad occasions in his life when he had resorted to prostitutes, the minimal, soulless dialogue which exposed the routine tedium of the transaction. He didn't think that he could face a whole evening of fencing innuendo with Gary, and decided it was time to own up to his real purpose in arranging the encounter.

"Listen," he began suddenly, "I didn't really fix to meet you this evening for a lot of small talk over dinner."

"No?" Gary Stane arched an eyebrow quizzically.

"No. I set up this meeting merely as a means to an end."

"Did you? I wonder why."

"Well, it's—"

"You don't have to tell me." Gary raised a hand to quiet Charles, and began to recite a well-known rubric. "The Intro/Outro Agency merely provides companions for social evenings. A drink, dinner, theatre, that sort of thing. That is all that the fee you pay secures, and at the end of the evening, when I have discharged my duties as your companion, we part, having both, I hope, had a good night out."

"I didn't mean—"

Again the hand was raised, and this time the voice was lowered. "Mind you, Charles, if we were to get on particularly well . . ."

Charles felt a pressure against his shin. He realized it came from Gary's leg and sat back, disguising the suddenness of his movement with a manufactured sneeze.

"Particularly well," Gary repeated, "then maybe the evening could continue in our own time. My own time, that is, outside my working hours. Of course, we'd have to negotiate a separate fee for that. But I'm sure we could come to some . . . arrangement. What hotel are you staying in?"

Charles took a deep breath. "I'm afraid that wasn't what I meant."

Gary's eyes narrowed. "Anything . . . unusual comes extra."

"No, listen. I've got you here under false pretences."

"What do you—"

"No, not under false pretences. I'm paying for your company and your conversation, and what I've paid entitles me to choose what that conversation is about."

"Ye-es," the boy conceded cautiously. A new understanding came into his eyes. "What sort of things does it excite you to talk about?"

"I want to talk about the Saturday before last, the evening before Yves Lafeu was murdered."

This at last brought some animation into Gary Stane's eyes. First came shock, then resentment, finally petulance.

"Are you a cop too?"

"You've talked to them?"

"They've talked to me."

"Well, I'm not one of them."

"Why should I believe that?"

"Because it's the truth. I am an actor called Charles Paris."

"Suppose I should be grateful that at least you used your own name," said Gary sarcastically. "What's your interest in it, anyway?"

"A friend of mine is Tristram Gowers' cousin. He doesn't believe that Tristram killed Yves, and he wants me to prove his cousin's innocence."

"Well . . ." Gary said. "No, I don't think you are a policeman."

"Meaning?"

"Meaning that they're all convinced that Yves was killed by Tristram."

"And what do you think?"

Gary shrugged without great interest. "It seems the obvious solution."

"Look, do you mind talking to me about all this?"

The boy shrugged again. "As you say, you've paid your money, so you can choose the subject."

"How well did you know Yves?"

"Hardly at all. Met him twice."

"The second occasion being the evening before he died?"

"Right."

"And the first being at the Sparta Club?"

"Done your homework, haven't you? Yes, I met him at the Sparta Club."

"Of which you are not a member."

"God, no. Way out of my league financially. No, a 'gentleman' took me there. Through the agency. He booked me. And when we were there, Yves came up and started chatting me up outrageously. I'm afraid the guy I was with got rather pissed off."

"Was Tristram there?"

"Yes. He wasn't in a wonderful mood either."

Charles felt embarrassed. "Did you and Yves, er, go off together?"

Gary smiled, enjoying his discomfiture. "Off to do naughty things together?"

"Yes."

"No. We just danced. It was a bit of fun. He was only behaving like that to get Tristram angry. I know the sort. Flirt like mad—they get some kind of charge out of it. Make the boyfriend furious and then have a lot of fun making it up. That must have been how their relationship worked." He stopped. "Until it went wrong."

"And that was really all that happened between you?"

"Really. I couldn't have gone off with him, anyway. I was with my client. Shouldn't really have danced like that, but I couldn't resist it." His face turned glum. "Had to pay for it."

"From the agency?"

"No, Maxine didn't get to hear about it."

So Charles had been right. The Maxine Ruttemann Agency and Intro/Outro were the same girl. But he didn't say anything, as Gary elaborated.

"But I had to pay for my client's silence. Go back with him to quite the vilest hotel in Paddington, where he insisted on doing things that . . . Well, some people have got the nastiest tastes."

"But, Gary, if your acquaintance with Yves was as slight as you say, why did he make such a fuss of you when you arrived at Tryst— greeting you like a long-lost lover and all that?"

Gary tutted with exasperation. "Don't you see? He was doing the same thing again—teasing Tristram, flirting, getting him furious. That sort of thing stimulated them, both of them."

Charles reached for his whisky glass, but it was empty. Gary was out of Campari too. Charles waved at the waiter and re-ordered.

"Tell me, Gary, how did you come to be at Tryst? Why did you go there?"

"Just a booking through the agency."

"To meet Mr Carruthers?"

"That's right. At eleven o'clock."

"You'd never heard of Mr Carruthers?"

"No." Gary Stane gave a twisted smile. "Very few of my clients use their real names."

"And you didn't know that Tryst would have stopped serving dinner by eleven o'clock?"

"Like the Sparta, love, Tryst is outside my usual range."

"And you didn't know that Yves worked there?"

"God, no. I knew nothing about him."

"And were you surprised when there was no Mr Carruthers waiting for you?"

"I wouldn't have been. Quite often turn up and find I'm alone. People make the booking and then lose their nerve. But in this case, I didn't know he wasn't there."

"What do you mean?"

"Well, the girl on the door said she'd check the book, and before she'd done that, Yves appeared . . . and then Tristram . . . and the furies were unleashed."

"Hmm." Charles picked his words carefully. "I don't suppose you know—"

Gary smiled triumphantly. "I know what you're going to ask."

"How?"

"You forget, I've been through all this with the police. You want to know the voice of the person who made the booking."

"That's right. Do you know?"

"Oh yes. Maxine took it. Very reliable memory, Maxine."

"Ah."

Gary smiled, a gentler smile than before. "Good girl, Maxine. We're getting married in the spring."

Charles's mouth fell open. "What?"

"God, you don't think I do it with men because I like it, do you? If there were the acting work about . . . or the dancing, I'd do that. As it is . . . well, we're saving up the deposit on a house."

Charles looked bewildered.

"Yes, I know, Charles, terrible, isn't it—the things people will do to make money."

"Oh, I don't know. I've recently been talking to someone about the chances of getting work charring."

"Hmm." Gary grimaced. "At least you can wear rubber gloves for that."

"But back to the booking," urged Charles.

"Yes. Of course. Well, Maxine remembered because it was such an unusual voice to be using the name 'Mr Carruthers'."

"What sort of voice—male or female?"

"Oh, male. And with a strong French accent."

"Oh. But I—"

"Don't you see? It must have been Yves himself. He set it up. Part of his teasing of Tristram. I mean, if you think about it, it was rather a coincidence that he should appear just as I arrived. But if he knew I was coming . . ."

"I hadn't thought of that."

"No. But that must have been it. That's what the police reckon, anyway. Just another of Yves's little games at Tristram's expense—only this one misfired."

They had their second drink and talked a little longer, but Gary had no more information to give. Eventually, with some awkwardness, Charles suggested that maybe they didn't bother with the rest of the planned evening.

Gary said that, so long as the agency fee was paid, he was quite happy to forego his dinner.

He looked more animated than he had all evening as he pocketed his twenty pounds and rose to leave. "Thanks. It's like being given a half-day off school," he said skittishly. Then he winked. "Maxine and I could do with an early night."

Chapter Nine

MONIQUE LAFEU WAS strangely unfeminine. It was as if her brother had appropriated the family ration of femininity and left her drained of sexuality. She was not ugly, but there seemed about her a coldness, a dullness even, that did not invite intimacy.

She was tall and big-boned, but there was no angularity or awkwardness in her movements. She walked, as she did everything, with short-tempered efficiency. The distinctive Gallic pout of her lips carried no message of passion, merely one of slight resentment, as if every external contact of her life was an imposition. Seeing her again, and remembering her at the reception counter of Tryst, Charles could visualize her in a few years in charge of a French restaurant, a looming presence at the cash-desk, keeping an unsmiling spider-watch over her diners.

Her manner was already proprietorial when they met that Tuesday morning at Tryst. She had suggested the venue, so presumably she had a key and had either sought or not bothered to seek police permission to use the premises.

Her resentful pout was marked, implying, even though she had set up the meeting, that Charles and O'Rourke's appearance was an intrusion. "Things will be a lot simpler," she began, after minimal formal greetings had been exchanged, "now they are both dead."

Her English was heavily accented, but fluent and easy to understand.

"This is a good setting for a restaurant," she went on, "and I think it should do very well. There is no need for all of the . . . what's the word you use? . . . *campness* which Yves brought to it."

Charles did not agree with that view. To his mind, much of the appeal of Tryst had been in the outrageousness of its owners. But he did not interrupt Monique.

"What makes a restaurant is not all of the . . . what do you call it? . . . set-dressing? It is just good food and efficient service."

"Were your parents in the restaurant business?" asked O'Rourke politely.

"Why do you ask?"

"Well, I just thought with Yves and you both going into—"

"No. My father is *épicier* . . . he owns a grocery store in Reims."

"So have they been here?"

Monique's eyes clouded with incredulity. "No. But if we may get on with our business . . ."

Though the nature of what she regarded as their business had not yet been defined, O'Rourke showed no curiosity about it. Indeed, he seemed unwilling to move the subject on, anxious for delay. Charles did not interfere, sensing that his friend had some plan of campaign.

"It must have been a terrible shock for you, Miss Lafeu," O'Rourke said formally. "To hear of the death of your brother."

She shrugged. "Of course. But people who live that sort of life are always at risk of such things. It is perhaps a punishment for what they do."

O'Rourke did not visibly bridle at this, though Charles knew it must have caused him annoyance. Instead, he went on, "How did you actually hear the news?"

"From the police."

"Here in England?"

"No, I was in Reims. I went for my vacation on the day after the restaurant closed. And then three days later I have to come back." She tutted and tossed her head back at the inconvenience.

"And did your parents come over too?"

"It was not necessary. There is no need for them to see . . . this place." The disapproval was undisguised. "They do not need to know everything. When the police release Yves's body, he will be buried in France. A terrible accident, a misfortune, the murder by a madman—that is all they need to know."

"You mean they didn't know that Yves lived with Tristram?"

"There was no need," Monique snapped.

"But if the police talk to them, it may come out."

"I hope the police will not talk to them. That is why I am here—to stop such talkings."

"But surely—"

"Anyway, this is not why we are here," Monique cut in abruptly.

"No. Why are we here?" asked Charles. He knew why he and O'Rourke were there, but he was interested to know why Monique had instigated the encounter.

She was not amused by his interruption and turned her cold eyes on him. "I do not know why *you* are here. Mr O'Rourke is here because I invited him to come and talk to me."

"Mr Paris is a friend and adviser to me. I wished him to be present."

O'Rourke's intervention received another toss of the head. "I will tell you why I wished you here. I heard you were trying to make contact with me. You telephoned one of the waiters, Mr O'Rourke."

"Yes."

"He told me. He told me some of the questions you asked him. He gave me the idea you were also investigating my brother's murder."

"Well . . ."

"There is nothing to investigate. The police have all the facts. Yves was killed by Tristram."

"But until Tristram's found—"

"Yves was killed by Tristram!" she repeated with surprising vehemence. "There is nothing else to think. And it is not good for the memory of the dead to investigate further."

"But when there are suspicious circumstances—"

"There are no suspicious circumstances, Mr O'Rourke. Tristram killed my brother, drove to Mas-de-Pouzard, and killed himself. This is not suspicious. It is wicked, yes, it is cruel, but it is very simple and straightforward."

O'Rourke was temporarily silenced by the vigour of her assault, so Charles decided it might be the moment for him to say something. "I'm sorry, I can't agree, Miss Lafeu. Until Tristram's body is found, there are many suspicious circumstances. And, unless he delivers a confession (if he is still alive) or confesses in a suicide note, those suspicions will remain."

"They will not! Frequently the bodies of *suicidés* are not found for many years. It is quite enough for my family to have had its tragedy and to have had the police interfering, without having other people busying themselves in our affairs."

"I am afraid," said Charles gently, "when people are murdered, that is the kind of thing that happens. You speak of the tragedy of *your* family," and, he reflected, without much emotion, "but there are other families too. Tristram Gowers was—is—O'Rourke's cousin."

"This is no reason to interfere in—"

"Oh, but it is." His interruption took the wind out of her sails, so Charles pressed on. "On the night Yves died, what time did you leave the restaurant?"

She was so surprised at the directness of the questioning that she replied with automatic docility. "I left with the rest of the staff . . . about two o'clock."

"No one stayed?"

"Only Yves and Tristram. We tidied up quickly. It was the beginning of the *vacances*." By now she had had time to feel affronted. "I do not know how you have the nerve to question me like this. I—"

"Listen," said Charles. "According to you, there were no suspicious circumstances that evening. But there were."

"For example?"

"All right. The young man, Gary Stane . . . You remember him?" Monique nodded curtly.

"When he came into this room at eleven o'clock that Saturday night, were you expecting him?"

"Of course not. Why should I?"

"If Yves had arranged for the boy to come, he might have told you so that you wouldn't turn him out. Did Yves tell you the boy was coming?"

Monique was silent, as if weighing up the advantages of various answers to this question. Charles was equally concerned. If Yves had warned his sister about Gary's expected arrival, then all had been as the police believed—the boy had been set up by Yves to antagonize his lover. And if that had happened, the case for any alternative interpretation of the murder was much weakened.

"No, Yves said nothing," Monique replied at last.

"In that case," Charles interposed quickly, "why did you let Gary in? He had no booking. You knew last orders had been given hours before. The kitchen was virtually closed. Why did you let him in?"

For the first time that morning, Monique looked confused.

Perhaps she was wishing she had said that Yves had arranged the encounter. That would have tied up the loose ends neatly; whereas now she appeared to be getting into an uncomfortable area of questioning.

"Come on—why?" Charles demanded. "You knew how the restaurant worked. If anyone else had walked in at that time of night, you would have said, 'Sorry, sir, we're closed.' Why didn't you do that with Gary Stane?"

"I did, but he still walked in."

Charles shook his head. "I was here that night. So was O'Rourke. We both saw exactly what happened."

Monique shrugged. "This is a waste of time. I have nothing to say."

"What a pity. If you told us your reason, we might get off your back. If you don't, well . . ." Charles decided it was his turn to have a shrug ". . . we're just going to get tha͟   ͟h more suspicious, aren't we?"

"All right," Monique conceded petulantly. "I will tell you. I did not know this Gary . . . whatever it is? I had never seen him before, but when he came in, I could tell . . . what he was."

You'd have been wrong, thought Charles, in response to the contempt of her tone.

"So I knew what might happen if Tristram and Yves met him, so I just let him in."

"You let him in deliberately to make trouble?"

"If you like."

"But why? Did you hate Yves?"

"No, I did not hate Yves." Now she spoke with more animation, perhaps more passion, than before. "I loved Yves as he was. When I was a child, when he was my big brother, then I loved him. But not after he met this Tristram. Then he is not my brother, he becomes something else."

"So it's Tristram you hate?"

"Perhaps. Tristram and what he made of Yves. They were wicked. It is good they are dead."

Monique did not seem embarrassed by what she had said. Her hard eyes took on a dreamy quality as she went on, "The restaurant will be better without them. It will be simple, ordinary French *cuisine*, but it will be very good. The best. It will be a place I will be proud for my parents to come to."

"This is assuming that you would be running it?" asked O'Rourke, who had been silent for some time.

"But of course. That is what I will do. I know enough now about the business. I am a good administrator. I will do well."

"And what makes you think it will be yours to run?"

"The restaurant?" She looked bewildered at O'Rourke's stupidity. "But of course it will be mine. My parents have no interests in England. They will let me run it."

"Suppose Tristram is still alive. What then?"

"Tristram is dead," she announced with uncontradictable assurance.

"If he is, then presumably his Will will be obeyed."

"I suppose so." She did not seem very interested in this. "If there is a Will. But Tristram had no family, anyway. So it will all come to us."

"No," said O'Rourke, suddenly forceful. "Tristram did make a Will, and he left everything to me."

Monique Lafeu gaped. When, finally, she could find speech, it was only a whisper. "No. No. But if that were true, then there was no reason for them to die."

Charles and O'Rourke sat over a second carafe of red wine in a Notting Hill Italian restaurant. "Difficult to say," said Charles. "She's an unusual woman."

"Well, she certainly seemed to hate her brother."

"And Tristram even more so."

"And she was very put out at the idea of my inheriting the restaurant."

"Yes, I don't think she believed you. But I bet she's talked to a solicitor by now."

"Yes, I bet she has, Charles." O'Rourke ran his fingers across the dome of his head, flattening the few hairs into place. "Certainly big enough."

"What, you mean big enough, strong enough, to have committed the murder?"

"Yes. Cold-blooded enough, too."

"Apparently. But you can't always judge—"

"She also went to France the day after Yves was killed."

"That was prearranged. Going to her parents."

"Oh yes. But if we're following your thesis of someone making Tristram drive down through France at gunpoint . . ."

"Hardly a thesis, more a random speculation."

"That's about all we can hope for at the moment in this case."

"Yes. Either random speculation . . . or the obvious solution."

"When Tristram is found and confesses, then I'll believe the obvious solution."

Charles sighed. O'Rourke looked troubled. "You are still with me, aren't you?"

"Oh yes. For what I'm worth, you have my full attention."

"Hmm." The collector circled a finger round the top of his wine-glass. "What are you doing for the next few days?"

"Nothing. Oh, well, I promised to take someone to an open audition tomorrow morning. Otherwise . . ."

"The 'rest' continues?"

"That's about it. Why do you ask?"

"Well, Charles, the thing that's stopping this investigation from progressing anywhere is the fact that Tristram has still not been found."

"Yes."

"But he is known to have driven all the way down to Mas-de-Pouzard, which is presumably where he was last seen. I want to go and look for him, Charles."

"What? You mean—"

"Yes. How do you fancy a trip to France?"

Chapter Ten

CHARLES MET HENRY on the Wednesday morning, outside the Shaftesbury Avenue exit from Piccadilly Circus Tube Station, as they had arranged. The open audition was not scheduled to start until ten, but, knowing how queues built up for that kind of occasion, he had suggested a nine o'clock meeting.

She looked as succulent as ever. Her hair was scraped back into a strict ballet-dancer's bun, which only accentuated the rounded youth of her face. She wore a yellow and black horizontally striped mini-dress over what presumably, from the matching sleeves and tights, was a purple leotard. Little gold boots completed the ensemble of what the television series *Fame* had told her a working actress would wear.

"Oh, hello, Charles. It's frightfully nice of you to turn up. I thought you might have forgotten."

"I said I'd be here." His voice was mildly aggrieved.

"Yes, I know. I'm sorry. It's just . . . well, some people say things and don't do them."

As they walked along Shaftesbury Avenue, she confessed that she felt "absolutely ghastly".

"Nerves?"

"Yes."

"Well, don't get it out of proportion. Remember, you're just going for the experience. Put out of your mind any thought that you might get a part."

"Yes, yes, of course." But there was a note of wistfulness in her voice. Her fantasies had clearly been working overtime, building images of the great producer out front recognizing her unique star quality, casting her in the lead, and setting her on a path of hitherto-unequalled success. It is every actor's dream, the dream of which none of them are ever quite cured. Even Charles, through his layers of cynicism, could still occasionally relapse into it.

So, if he was going to let her down, he knew it would have to be done gently. "I mean, these auditions won't be for the principals. Those will have been sorted out. They'll just be looking for boys and girls for the chorus. A lot of those may have been sorted out already too. These open auditions are often just a nod in the direction of democracy. I'm afraid real life is very rarely like *Chorusline*."

"No, no, of course not." But he had not eradicated the little fantasy bloom of hope in Henry's voice.

"Did Bertram tell you roughly what the form is?" asked Charles, leaving dream-demolition aside for a moment.

"No." Again the glow that Bertram Pride's name seemed always to bring came, on cue, to her cheeks. "No, no, I haven't actually seen much of Bertram this week. He doesn't even know I'm going to this."

Charles made no more comment than an "Oh", then continued, "Well, basically what happens is you go and join the queue at the stage door. Then when you get backstage, someone'll take your name and agent's name—oh, you haven't got one."

"No."

"Well, never mind. Then they'll probably ask if you're Equity— did it specify Equity in the ad.?"

"It said 'Equity preferred'."

"Well, that's better than 'Equity only'. It means they might take on a beginner who was exceptionally good. Depends whether it's for West End or a tour. And again whether it's a Number One tour or not . . ."

Henry looked puzzled, but Charles decided not to depress her further with the complexities of his union's regulations. "Anyway, if they ask about Equity, say you've nearly got your full card. That'll imply you've only got a few more weeks to do."

"But what if I'm actually offered a part?"

Oh dear, the fantasies were tenacious. "Cross that bridge when you come to it," said Charles kindly.

"And then what happens?"

"When you finally get onstage?"

"Yes."

"Well, you do your bit—or at least as much of it as they'll let you. They're always running way behind time, and they always apologize that they have to be brief, but usually you're allowed to get a few words out before they stop you. You have got something prepared, I assume?"

"Oh yes."

"Good."

"I've done a Portia speech."

"What!" Charles stopped dead in the middle of the pavement.

"You know, Portia, *Merchant of Venice*."

"Yes, I know Portia."

"'The quality of mercy is not strain'd', that one."

"Henry, you can't do that."

"What?" She looked distressed. "But I do do it well—really. I played Portia in the school play, and then when I was at college my Drama Tutor said it was a frightfully good audition piece."

"Where were you at college?"

"A place in Bath. You probably wouldn't have heard of it," Henry replied, slightly evasively.

"What, a drama school?"

"Well, we did a lot of drama." Her little chin was set defiantly.

"Hmm." Charles got the picture. Some kind of high-class finishing school, offering its own totally worthless diploma in performing arts. Henry was even less qualified to be an actress than he had thought. But she looked so vulnerable that he could not restrain his benevolence. "They really should have taught you about auditions. The important thing is always to have something suitable prepared. I mean, this is for a musical—no one's going to want to hear your favourite gems from Shakespeare."

In spite of his gentle tone, Henry looked crushed.

"I'm sorry, love, but you did ask me to give you a few tips, and this is exactly the sort of thing you ought to know. At least I've saved you the embarrassment of going up onstage and making a fool of yourself."

"Yes, Charles. Thank you. I just thought, you know, they'd hear the speech and then, if they thought I was good enough, they'd sort of ask me about singing and that sort of thing."

"They don't have time. I'm afraid it's straight on and off. Some'll get recalled, but they'll have had to show basic dancing and singing skills first. Incidentally, another tip. If you are recalled, make sure the request is made vaguely publicly. If the director suggests discussing the part further at his flat later in the evening, be wary."

"Oh. You mean . . . ?" Obviously it wasn't just the mention of Bertram Pride; it was anything connected with sex that made Henry blush. "So what should I have prepared for this audition?" she asked contritely.

"A song. Do you have any music?"

She shook her head.

"But you can sing?"

"Oh yes. I was taught music for ages and ages."

"So you can sight-read?"

"Yes."

"Then all is not lost. Come on, let's find a music shop and get you something you can sing."

In the music shop it turned out that she had once been in a school production of *South Pacific*, so they homed in on *I'm Gonna Wash That Man Right Out Of My Hair*. It wasn't as up to date as it might have been, but at least she was familiar with the tune.

"And what else will happen?" Henry asked, as they neared the King's Theatre.

"There'll probably be a choreographer there. He may take you through a few steps, probably in groups. Or perhaps they'll hear you sing first and only select a few for the dancing. It depends."

"Gosh, what are all these people doing?" asked Henry.

"I've a horrible feeling they're the queue," said Charles.

"But we're nowhere near the stage door of the King's."

"No. Look, you join the queue in case. I'll go and reconnoitre."

It was the queue. The youth of those waiting, the leotards, the wild clothes, the heightened quality of the conversation all gave Charles the message long before he had rounded the fourth corner to see the "Stage Door" sign ahead.

It was going to be a long wait.

So it proved. The queue moved with agonizing slowness. Lunchtime passed. Charles snuck off and bought himself a ham roll, but Henry said she didn't feel hungry. She didn't feel thirsty either, and Charles spent opening hours in agony filing slowly past a pub, feeling that in some obscure way it would be unchivalrous to leave her and go inside for a few pints. He had said he would look after Henry and that was what he was going to do.

By three-thirty they were inside the building, and then the queue seemed to stop completely for an hour. Charles wondered what the reason might be—the discovery of a new star, somebody throwing a scene, or the producer and director taking a late lunch-break. He looked anxiously ahead, trying to gauge how many there were to go before Henry. Auditions of that sort were often badly mismanaged and, if it were to happen, it wouldn't have been the first time that people who had been queuing for eight hours were told to come back the next day.

But the log-jam was sorted out and the slow forward progress recommenced. A harassed-looking young man took Henry's details. He had too much on his mind to be worried by her lack of experience, and so that hurdle was passed.

Soon they were in earshot of the stage, and could hear what was being sung. As Charles had feared, audition pieces were keeping well up with fashion. A lot of the hopefuls would have recently been in work and tended to perform items from shows they had just finished. Stephen Sondheim and *Chorusline* were favourites; and a lot had clearly been studying Andrew Lloyd-Webber LPs. But Henry wouldn't sound completely on her own. So many reps had been playing safe and reviving old musicals in the last few years that there was a sprinkling of Rodgers and Hammerstein, even smatterings of Franz Lehar, Rudolf Friml and Sigmund Romberg.

Eventually they could see the stage, and Charles felt Henry's tension grow. The boys and girls who auditioned had all worked professionally before. Their notes might wobble, their vowels lurch transatlantically, their movements betray mannerism rather than rhythm, but they all had the minimal gloss that comes from having worked before a paying audience. Charles, who knew nothing of Henry's performing abilities, felt anxious for her.

Mind you, even the professionals weren't getting long to show their paces. The very good ones were allowed to get through a verse and chorus; the less competent were chopped off after their verse by the anonymous shout from the auditorium. It was like a parody of a

Nazi death camp, seeing how long each aspirant could survive before being led meekly off to execution.

At last Henry was next. The young man preceding her had the nerve to object to being cut short. The voice from the auditorium apologized that they had to be brief. The young man said they wouldn't recognize talent if it came and peed over them. He added that the accompanist had as much sense of rhythm as a bag of sick, and, snatching his music from the piano, stormed off the stage.

Whether this prelude would help Henry or not, Charles couldn't judge. Certainly she looked very pretty as she walked onstage. And, considering the circumstances, very assured. Her background and finishing school may not have given her much drama training, but it had given her poise.

She handed her music to the accompanist, who looked at her with the weary expression of a man who has already played the beginning of *Don't Cry For Me, Argentina* over fifty times that day and has just been compared to a bag of sick. He sat at the piano and, without preamble, launched into the opening bars of *I'm Gonna Wash That Man Right Out Of My Hair*.

Henry looked thrown, as if she had expected to make some announcement, or to be greeted by the faceless voices out front. Charles peered through the curtain. Under the lip of the Circle he could see nothing, except for the little glow of a light over an improvised table set on two rows of seats. The faces of producer, director, perhaps choreographer, secretary and casting director were invisible in the shadow.

But Henry came in on her note. She had a clear, pure voice, and sang very simply, without the mannered emphases of the previous auditionees. Hers was really a drawing-room voice, rather than a stage voice, but it seemed to fill the auditorium.

And she did look so pretty.

For a moment Charles wondered if the miracle was about to happen, if her dream was about to be fulfilled, if she was to be spotted and rocketed to stardom.

She had just started on the chorus when her sentence was pronounced.

"Thank you," called the nameless voice from the stalls. "Sorry, love. We have to be brief."

Charles was worried that she might have been depressed by the experience. She was preoccupied as they left the theatre, dawdled as if waiting for something. (The something in question, Charles feared, was the Hollywood scene of a boyishly handsome producer rushing after her and saying, "I can't let a girl like you go. You gotta work for me.")

But no such scenario developed and, once they were out of sight of the theatre, Henry seemed to relax. "Gosh," she said, "I'm absolutely ravenous. Always feel like that after a performance—it must be release of tension."

Charles didn't argue with her definition of a performance, but suggested that they wander down to Covent Garden and have a cup of tea somewhere. (It was still an hour until the pubs opened.)

"No, no, you must come back to the flat," urged Henry. "You've been so kind to me, Charles, really. Come back and have a drink and a bit of fodder."

Then she hailed a cab with a style and readiness that few unemployed actresses of her age would have commanded, and gave an address in Sloane Street.

Inside the cab, Charles dared to ask her what she had thought of the audition.

"Oh, it was really A.1. I mean, v.g., absolutely."

"You weren't disappointed?"

"Gosh, no. It was just frightfully nice being, you know, with actors, in a really professional situation. I mean, it sort of gave me a feeling of it. You know, the experience will help. I must be ready to go through any number of disappointments before I get where I want to be." Then, turning her wonderful wide eyes on Charles, she said, "The Theatre's a cruel mistress, you know."

"Yes," agreed Charles, desperately controlling a twitching at the corners of his mouth.

The cab drew up outside an expensive block of flats in Sloane Street and Henry paid off the driver as if by instinct. Charles passed no comment on the elegance of the facade, or the wide hall with its uniformed commissionaire, or the plushly carpeted lift. He said nothing until they were inside the flat itself, whose punctiliously designed interior matched the luxury of the block. He looked out over the highly-priced roofs of Kensington, and allowed himself a "Very nice."

"Yes, not bad, is it? Of course, it's not mine."

"No?"

"Oh gosh, no. Hobby and I are really just squatters here."

"Squatters?"

"Yes. Well, I mean Daddy owns it, but we're just squatters."

"I see."

"Could you fancy a drink?"

Charles admitted that he probably, at a pinch, could.

"Great. After a day like today, I wouldn't mind getting a bit chateaued. Got some fizz in the fridge, that be okay?"

"Fine," said Charles, not quite sure what the "fizz" would be.

"And if I rustle up the odd smoked salmon sarnie, be okay?"

"Fine."

Soon they were sitting over the sandwiches, neat in fresh brown bread, and the "fizz", which proved to be a very acceptable non-vintage champagne, and Henry was enthusing about how grateful she was to Charles and what she planned to do next to further her career and how she was really prepared to work amazingly hard and wouldn't mind reverses and was really prepared to stick at it until she made it. Charles supplied the relevant agreements and encouragements and drank and thought how amazingly pretty she was.

Their idyll was rudely interrupted. The door to the living room was flung open and, framed in it, stood a stocky young man in his mid-twenties. He wore a blazer and regimental tie, had very short hair and a very red face.

Henry's sandwich plate crashed to the floor as she stood up, aghast. "James!"

"Yes, James," the young man confirmed. His voice carried the authority of many generations' shouting at grouse-beaters. "And what have you to say for yourself, eh?"

"How on earth did you get in?" asked Henry weakly.

"Met Hobby in the hall. She waited for the lift. I came up by the stairs. Thought I'd give you a little surprise. And I jolly well did, didn't I? I never thought I'd actually burst in and find you here with your elderly lover."

Charles cleared his throat. "I think you're getting the wrong end of the stick."

"Oh, you mean you're not an actor?" asked the young man pugnaciously.

"Well, yes, I am, but—"

"See!" The young man looked round the flat, as if to support his case. "And do you deny that your name is Bertram Pride?"

"Yes, I do. My name's Charles Paris."

The red brow wrinkled as this piece of information was digested. Then a new roar burst out. "Good God, Henry! You mean there's more than one of them?"

"No, James, Charles is just a friend."

"Huh! Come on, give me credit for something between the ears. That's the oldest line in the book. I told your father you'd go to the bad if you came up to London. You know, you should never have left Gloucestershire, young lady."

"Look, could I explain . . . ?" Charles began.

"You keep out of this! Now listen, Henry, I want to know what's what. I'd have come sooner, but I've been on a training course. And let me tell you, it hasn't been much fun having my girl-friend's name plastered all over the gossip columns. Some pretty nasty remarks passed in the mess, let me tell you. Honestly, I turn my back for a fortnight and find you've turned into some backstage groupie!"

"No, it's not like that, James. Let me explain—"

"Don't need your explanations! I'd just like to know what this succession of ageing matinee idols think they're doing seducing my girl left, right and centre and—"

"If I'm meant to be one of the succession," Charles interposed firmly, "you are way off target. I have just been giving Henry some advice on her career."

"Huh!" snorted James.

"It's true," said a new voice. Hobby, a sardonic smile on her face, had appeared in the doorway behind the young officer.

"Oh." James, momentarily discomfitted, stepped aside to let her come into the room. She put down her brief case, kicked off her shoes, and flopped into a chair, whence she watched the proceedings with enthusiasm.

"Well, I'm sorry if I've slandered you," James said grudgingly to Charles. Then he rounded on Henry again. "But what about this Bertram Pride? Do you deny that you've been going around with him?"

"No, I don't. But I've only been out with him for a few meals, discotheques, that sort of thing. It was part of our agreement, James. We did say we should both be free to go out with other people."

"Go out, okay!" stormed the young officer. "But not sneak off for dirty weekends at country cottages! There was nothing about that in our agreement!"

"It wasn't like that, James. Really."

"What, so the gossip column got it wrong?"

"Yes."

"What, there never was any idea of you going off to this louse's cottage?"

"Well, yes, there was an idea. I mean, we had discussed it. We had intended to."

"Exactly as the gossip column said."

"Yes. But . . ." Henry looked torn, embarrassed. She glanced at her sister, as if wishing that Hobby were out of the room. But she couldn't avoid the truth. James's bristling fury had to be answered.

"We had planned to go . . ." Henry's voice was very small. "But, when it came to it, we didn't."

"James is all right, really," said Henry. "You didn't see him at his best. He can be frightfully good company."

She and Charles were sitting outside a Covent Garden wine bar the next day. She had agreed readily when he had suggested meeting to talk. She wanted to apologize for the haste with which James had hurried him out of the flat.

"You've known him a long time?"

"Since we were tinies, yes. Well, since I was tiny. He's six years older than me. And, you know, our parents are great friends and . . . oh, I dare say I'll end up marrying him."

"But not yet."

"No. You see, one of the great things about coming up to London, I mean, apart from getting into the theatre, was, you know, to meet a few people other than James."

"You didn't have a big split-up?"

"No. It was just . . he was the only boy I'd ever been out with and, you know, I sort of felt I ought to meet some other people rather than going straight into marriage."

"Reasonable."

"Yes. Anyway, James said, okay, if that's what I really wanted, then I should do it. I mean, he's in the army, based in Scotland. I don't see that much of him, anyway, so it wouldn't make a great deal of difference to him."

"So you agreed that you could both go out with other people, so long as nothing got serious?"

"Yes. So long as . . . well . . . there was nothing, you know . . ." She blushed, so Charles knew she was talking about sex.

"I understand."

"Anyway, James thought the same about my coming up to London as Daddy did. Neither of them think I'll stick it. They both think I'll be back in Gloucestershire—and probably married to James—before the year's out."

"And will you?"

"No." Henry jutted her chin out with determination.

"Which brings us to . . . Bertram Pride," said Charles lightly.

"Yes." Henry paused, mustering her ideas. "It's complicated. I met him at a party, and, you know, he was jolly nice to me, and, well, I was flattered. I mean, he is a famous face. And, you know, him being older than me . . . well, I never thought someone of that age would be interested in someone like me."

Then you are genuinely unaware of just how attractive you are, thought Charles. Really, it would be sad to see something so pretty and so charming wasted on an upper-class blusterer like James.

"So, anyway, Bertram started taking me out and, you know, he's good company. He knew the right places to go and everyone recognized him, and we had a good time. And at that stage there wasn't anything, you know . . ." Her blush told Charles exactly what she meant. "But then he started talking about this country cottage, and how he must take me down there, and well, I knew exactly what he meant."

"Yes. So how did you react?"

"Well, part of me was drawn to the idea. I mean, I wasn't in love with him, but, you know, he was attractive and he seemed kind. And also I suppose I was swayed by him being famous and liking the idea of having an affair with someone famous . . . And perhaps even, selfishly, thinking he could help me in the theatre. So I sort of . . . didn't say no."

"Which he interpreted as meaning yes?"

She nodded. "And then, before I knew it, other people seemed to know we were going to the cottage and I thought, well, why not? And then there was Hobby . . ."

She tailed off.

"What had Hobby got to do with it?"

"Well, Hobby's a bit strait-laced, and I . . . told her I was going off with Bertram."

"To shock her?"

Henry looked full in his face, appreciative of his understanding. "Yes. A bit of that, yes. But, having told Hobby, having sort of made a stand about it, I thought I had to go through with it."

"But, in the event you didn't?"

"No. I lost my nerve. You see, Bertram and I were meant to be going straight down in my car after that dinner at Tryst . . . you know, when I first met you."

Charles nodded.

"And I felt sort of okay about it, because Bertram had said that, you know, there wouldn't be any . . ." She blushed furiously, but managed to bring out the word, "sex."

"But then, in the car, after we'd left the restaurant, well, it was clear that I had misunderstood him."

"Ah. So he *was* planning to spirit you off for a dirty weekend?"

Henry nodded. "And I sort of thought of James, and I knew that I didn't love Bertram, and I thought . . . well, I was scared."

"You mean it wasn't the sort of thing you'd done very often."

She looked very shame-faced, and Charles could only just hear her say, "Ever."

"I see." He looked at her and felt pity, pity for the pressures on a young girl which made her apologize for her virginity. "So what happened?"

"I'm afraid we had a row. Bertram was pretty angry. After a time he just left me."

"What do you mean?"

"He stormed out of the car and said he was going to get a cab home."

"So what did you do?"

"Well . . ." She looked even more miserable. "This sounds daft, but in fact I didn't dare go back to the flat. You see, having told Hobby, having made such an issue of it with Hobby, I just couldn't go back."

Having witnessed the competitive edge between the two sisters, Charles could understand this.

"So what did you do?"

"I drove around for a bit, just aimlessly, trying to decide where I should go. There are various chums whose floors I could have crashed out on, but, well, they all know each other and . . ."

"And you didn't want to lose face? You wanted to maintain the illusion that you had gone off with Bertram."

"Yes." She was nearly crying. "I thought it'd give me some sort of cachet with them. I don't know why. Whereas all it has got me is the most frightful row with James."

"Is he still furious with you?"

"Well, not quite so bad. He took me out to dinner last night and we got things a bit sorted out. But he's very hurt."

Charles pulled the subject back to what interested him. "So where did you spend that night?"

"In the car. I know, daft, but I did."

"Where?"

"Well, that was even dafter. I drove round in circles, and found that I'd ended up near Tryst again. I suppose I was vaguely looking for Bertram, thinking he might still be hanging around there for me."

"And was he?"

123

"No, of course not. So I parked there and spent an extremely uncomfortable night, dozing intermittently. The next day I drove down into the country and came back on the Sunday evening, pretending to Hobby that I'd actually spent the weekend with Bertram Pride."

Charles felt excitement welling inside him. "So in fact you spent the entire night parked outside Tryst?"

"Well, not exactly outside. Round the corner. Just by the entrance to the mews at the back."

Even better. "And you say you didn't sleep well?"

"On and off. Not much."

"And did you see any comings and goings from the mews?"

"Yes, I saw a few cars and things."

She spoke with her usual innocence, unaware of the importance of her words.

"Tell me what you saw?" asked Charles, trying to contain the agitation in his voice.

"Well, I think by the time I got there, all of the people eating dinner must have gone. But then there were a few cars and motor-bikes and a few people on foot who all came out of the mews about the same time. They woke me, they were calling out goodbyes to each other."

"Would that have been about two o'clock?"

"Round then, yes."

The staff, as Monique had said.

"Anything else?"

"I was woken up later by a car going out. It was going fast, the tyres screeched."

"What make was it?"

"A Volvo."

"Did you see the driver?"

"Only got an impression. Sort of lots of silver hair. I thought it was probably the proprietor . . ."

"Tristram Gowers?"

"That's right."

"You couldn't see whether there was anyone else in the car?"

Henry shook her head. "It was very loaded up in the back."

"Any idea what time that was?"

"I seem to remember looking at my watch and seeing it was just after half-past three."

Right on schedule for the six-thirty ferry at Dover.

Charles felt weary. He had built up so many different pictures of what had happened, and now he had a witness to confirm the police's reconstruction of events. Tristram Gowers had driven off at three-thirty. The idea that he was doing so while held at gunpoint by some hidden murderer in the back of the car now seemed fanciful.

"Thanks, Henry," he said wryly. "Don't suppose you saw anything else?"

"No cars, no."

"I was afraid that would be the answer."

"But I did see someone on foot."

"What!" Charles sat bolt upright. "Who? When?"

"Just before three it must have been. I saw someone walk into the mews."

"Did you see them come out?"

Henry shook her head. "I think I dozed off, though. They may have come out."

"And who was it?" asked Charles.

"I couldn't see the face," Henry replied, "but it was a woman. A tall woman."

Chapter Eleven

CONTINENTAL TRAVEL IN the company of Bartlemas and O'Rourke was conducted in some style. They drove in Bartlemas's vintage Lagonda, a silver monster which drew admiring glances on the road and seemed to ensure an obsequious welcome at the château-hotels they favoured with their custom.

They also ate on the way. In spite of the serious nature of their mission, they allowed the trip to be a little *tour gastronomique*, and it was a long time since Charles had eaten so much delectable food or drunk so much fine wine. Philip Marlowe, working on expenses, never had it so good.

They did not travel by the same route that the Volvo had taken. Their aim was not a reconstruction of that particular journey; for them the interest lay at the destination, in the house at Mas-de-Pouzard. So, rather than taking the Dover-Calais crossing, they had gone Southampton-Cherbourg and driven down (with detours in the cause of gastronomy) through Tours, Poitiers and Limoges.

When Charles looked at the map of France, he wondered why Tristram had chosen the other route. It seemed to involve more driving through less attractive countryside. He also noted, and wondered whether there was any significance in the fact, that it passed nearer to Reims. There was something important, he felt, in the relationship between Yves and his parents. Or, if not that, in the relationship between Monique and her parents.

But, when he raised the question of the route, O'Rourke explained it away instantly. Tristram had always been an exceptionally bad sailor, and so they always crossed by the shortest way. He would rather spend more time at the wheel than more time on the sea.

The countryside glowed with hazy warmth as they moved further south. Though it was mid-September, and the evening chill set in earlier, the sun at noon was still blisteringly hot. After a summer in London, where the sun is rarely more than a dusty inconvenience, Charles felt his body begin to relax with the therapy of the warm air.

But as they neared their destination, as the domesticated, anglicized scenery of the Dordogne gave way to the wilder, more ragged contours of the Lot-et-Garonne, the mood of the party sobered. Yves's death and the unknown fate of Tristram began to preoccupy them.

And, as so often happened, Charles's mood became dislocated from its immediate cause, and he found himself thinking of Frances. Partly it was being in France. The last time had been with her, many years before, when their marriage was first beginning to show signs of splitting. They had had four days of eating, drinking and sex along the Loire, four days when, removed from the humdrum daily life which their relationship could not tolerate, it had seemed that they might, after all, stay together forever. Back in England, reality had marched back in and they had been separated within a month.

But, in France again, Charles felt himself manipulated by the cheating regrets of nostalgia, went through the pointless circle of "if only"s, and speculated, worrying at the idea like a hangnail, whether Frances had been to the Loire with David.

The gastronomic dilatoriness of their progress meant that it was the evening of the third night when they passed through the medieval walls of Cahors. They checked in to a Michelin-recommended hotel in the town and settled down to yet another memorable meal. But they were all subdued. The next day they would go out to Mas-de-Pouzard. And, now that they were so close, they did not know what they were looking for there, or how they would set about finding it.

The next day summer gave a sudden late spurt and it promised to be hotter than ever.

Mas-de-Pouzard reminded Charles of the old schoolboy joke:

"What is the strangest town in England?"

"Diss."

"Why?"

"Because, when you get near it, the town Diss appears."

Mas-de-Pouzard also seemed to disappear as they came close to it. It was marked on the Michelin map, and they followed signposts along increasingly narrow tracks towards it, but then the signposts seemed to run out and they found themselves coming back to more major roads. A few kilometres further on there were signposts pointing back to "Mas-de-Pouzard".

"Well, we seem to have missed it . . ." said O'Rourke.

"But there was nothing there . . ." objected Bartlemas.

"No church . . ."

"No sign by the roadside . . ."

"No bar . . ."

"Nothing . . ."

"Still, we'd better go back . . ."

"No alternative . . ."

This time they stopped on the winding road in the middle of the hills at a point they reckoned to be equidistant between the nearest signposts in either direction. They had passed no road wider than a cart track and the only sign of human habitation was a small shack with scraps of blue fertilizer sacks hanging at its windows. There was no one in sight, but a few chickens scratching around suggested that it might be occupied.

"I'll see if there's anyone there." Charles got out of the car and walked towards the shack. Although the Lagonda was open-topped, it was only when they stopped that he could feel the full strength of the sun. He was sweating by the time he reached the paintless front door.

Knocking produced no reaction, but, wandering round the back, he found an old man tending a vegetable patch without great urgency.

Charles greeted him. The actor's French had once been quite good, and he found that a few days back in France had sharpened it considerably.

The old man straightened up and looked at Charles without curiosity. He wore blue overalls which had faded almost to brown; his face had the texture and colour of a walnut shell, and his teeth were reduced to three nicotine-stained stumps.

Yes, he confirmed, this was Mas-de-Pouzard.

Charles said he was looking for the house of Tristram Gowers. The old man shook his head. Or Yves Lafeu? Another dubious shake.

The English people, said Charles. Ah, the English. The old man gave a strange little limp-wristed gesture. Yes, said Charles.

"You are police?" asked the old man.

"No."

"But you want to find the house?"

"Yes."

The old man digested this for a moment. "I have the key," he announced at length. "You want me to let you in?"

"Well, yes, that would be wonderful. Wouldn't the police mind?"

The old man spat in the dust, but not vindictively. It was just a conversational gesture. "The police do not care. One of these men kills the other in England, comes here, kills himself. They are English, the police do not care."

The old man collected the key from inside his shack and accompanied Charles to the car. He found the Lagonda very funny. He found Bartlemas and O'Rourke, in matching Hawaiian shirts, powder blue slacks and espadrilles, even funnier. Every time they spoke, as he directed them along a cart track to the brow of a hill, the old man laughed out loud. But again there was no offence in his laughter.

As they came over the top of the hill, the first thing they saw was the river. The suddenness of the view was breathtaking. Cliffs fell away beneath them to the wide expanse of water reflecting the blue of the sky. Dark green trees mirrored themselves along the bank. On the far side a plain ran through the haze to the dark bulk of further hills.

Next they saw the house. It was an old farm-house built in pale grey stone, its low-pitched roofs covered in curved pinkish tiles. In front was a small covered courtyard from which stone steps mounted to a first-floor door. Under the eaves a row of black holes opened into the pigeon-loft. The building gave a Roman impression, like an illustration from a children's history book.

And in front of it still stood parked Tristram Gowers' Volvo.

The old man let them in through double doors on the courtyard level. Inside the house was cool, but it did not have the mustiness of a building that has been long unoccupied. It was beautifully decorated. Even a quick glance showed that no expense had been spared to bring the interior design up to the standard of the London flat.

"Is it rented out when the owners are not here?" asked Charles.

The old man nodded assent.

"We can't thank you enough for letting us in . . ." said Bartlemas in his acceptable French.

"No, it's so kind . . ." said O'Rourke in his almost acceptable French.

The old man roared with laughter. Then, asking them to drop the key in to him when they left, and refusing offers of a lift back to the road, he trudged out into the blinding sunlight. As he dwindled in the brightness, they could still hear him laughing. It was obviously a long time since he had had such a good laugh.

"Well, we've got here . . ." said Bartlemas.

"Yes, we've got here . . ." agreed O'Rourke.

"The question is . . ."

"What do we do now?"

"Now," said Charles Paris, "we search the place."

They were not the first to have done the job. The contents of the house were not disordered, but some items had been moved and replaced in a slightly illogical way. This must have been the work of the French police, who, although, according to the old man, they had little interest in a murder in London, had gone through the motions of a search. Or maybe the Scotland Yard men who had been out had done the job more seriously.

The fact of the earlier searches made it unlikely that Charles's party was going to find much. The chances of coming across Tristram's body strung up from a beam in the pigeon-loft were slender. But they still felt it was worth going through everything. There might be some clue to what Tristram had done when he reached the house and before he disappeared.

The Volvo had been emptied, and it didn't look as if this had been the result of Tristram's meticulous unpacking. The way the contents were spread out on the floor of the dining-room suggested that this had been the work of the French or English police. The suitcases had been opened and their contents riffled through, and the other items were arranged in little piles according to the categorizing instincts of some bureaucratic mind. While Bartlemas and O'Rourke searched the upper storey and the outbuildings, Charles went through this equipment for the holiday that never happened.

On the table were the couple's travel documents and passports. Charles looked inside both of the latter. Yves's was French, and the photograph was a good one, capturing both the beauty and the mischievous insolence of its original. Tristram's was also a good likeness, though his face, with its props of silver toupé, moustache and large glasses, as usual just looked like that of an Identikit restaurateur.

Charles checked both passports. There were no recent stamps for entry into France. But, as he knew from his own experience of a few days previously, passports very rarely get stamped for people crossing the Channel.

He looked at the rest of the luggage.

The most interesting pile was made up largely of books of pornographic pictures. These were not private blackmail photographs, but professionally produced books for specialized tastes. Needless to say, the speciality in this case proved to be homosexual.

But it was the other items on the pile that attracted Charles's attention. There were a pot of vaseline and two battery-operated vibrators.

And a woman's lipstick.

He called Bartlemas and O'Rourke into the dining-room and showed what he had found.

"Well, the vaseline, obviously. And the books, well . . ."

"I mean, if that's what Tristram and Yves *enjoyed* . . ."

"As they say over here, *chacun à son goût* . . ."

"And far be it from us to criticize the tastes of . . ."

"Anyone. Oh, far be it . . ."

"And the vibrators . . . well, again . . ."

"If that's what turned them on . . ."

"Well, exactly . . ."

"It wasn't really those I was interested in. It was this." Charles held up the lipstick between finger and thumb. He knew he shouldn't really be putting fingerprints on anything, but he had the feeling that the police investigation, certainly from the French side, and probably from the English too, was all sewn up, bar the formalities. "Now, the cop who sorted through this lot had a tidy mind, and I reckon all the stuff he put in this pile was . . . what shall I call it? . . . homosexual impedimenta?"

"What a charming phrase . . ."

"Enchanting . . ."

"And so *tasteful*, Charles . . ."

"And he obviously thought, in the simple way of policemen—homosexual equals transvestite, therefore they had the lipstick for their own uses."

The two heads shook as one.

"Not Tristram and Yves, no . . ."

"Not in a . . ."

"Million years . . ."

"No . . ."

"The general public does have very bizarre ideas of what gay people get up to . . ."

"Totally bizarre . . ."

"I mean of course there are the ones who're effeminate and who dress up in women's clothes, but not Tris and Yves . . ."

"Never . . ."

"No . . ."

"Good," said Charles. "Now all this stuff came out of the Volvo. We know how neat Tristram was. There is no way this lipstick would have been lying in the car before he packed. So if it didn't belong to him or to Yves, it must have belonged to someone else who travelled in the car after the murder."

"Yes," said O'Rourke. "And, at the risk of stating the obvious, presumably that someone was a woman."

Bartlemas and O'Rourke had reached the hardly surprising conclusion that Tristram's body was not on the premises. They had even lifted the metal cover off the old well, but found a metal grille set into the walls that would have prevented the passage of a corpse.

In spite of this, Charles continued to prowl round the house. While the others went off to the nearest town to buy bread, pâté and wine, he continued his search. Buoyed up by the discovery of the lipstick, he was now confident that he would find something else, some other clue that would explain the mysteries of Yves's death and Tristram's disappearance.

Their bedroom was the best room in the house. Glass doors opened on to a balcony, from which it felt that one could dive straight down into the waters of the Lot.

The bed was made, but the formality of its clean sheets had not been disturbed. They had presumably been put on by the maid who looked after the house between lets, perhaps the wife or daughter of the old man who had let them in.

There was no sign in the room that Tristram had entered it. Indeed, except for the signs of police activity, there was no indication that anyone had been in any part of the house since the last let. Maybe Tristram, after his long drive to Mas-de-Pouzard, had never made it inside.

This thought fed the theory that was beginning to take shape in Charles's mind.

In a drawer of the dressing-table he found a photograph album. It contained a selection of pictures from Tristram's and Yves's lives, mostly from their separate lives, before they became a couple. Many of the photographs shoved haphazardly behind the transparent film were of theatrical productions, showing a younger, pre-toupé Tristram in a variety of costumes, or Yves frozen in a series of dances. Mixed with these were childhood photographs of both of them, family groups, holiday snaps. It seemed like an attempt to marry the lives both had led before they met.

There was even, to Charles's surprise, a picture of Tristram with Zoë. The clothes and the poses gave away that it was from a production of Shakespeare. Zoë stood with page-boy haircut, dressed in a tunic and high boots, while beside her a balding Tristram crouched in motley, carrying the zany of a Shakespearean clown.

Charles felt fairly confident he could identify the scene. *Twelfth Night*. Beginning of Act Three.

Enter Viola, and Clown with a tabor.

VIOLA: Save thee, friend, and thy music. Dost thou live by the tabor?

CLOWN: No, sir, I live by the church . . .

The desperate unfunniness of the Clown's jokes was seared into Charles's memory. He had once had the misfortune to play the part. He always tried to avoid Shakespeare's funny men, knowing just how excruciatingly their humour fails with a modern audience. But on this particular occasion he had failed to duck it. To compound his agony, the director had been of the school that thought if the cast laughed enough at the jokes, the audience would eventually prove suggestible and join in. He was horribly wrong, and Charles had had to spend a miserable time roaring his head off about cheveril gloves and pilchards, while the audience shuffled in embarrassed silence. It had been a very lonely experience. And it hadn't impressed the critics much either. The *Bristol Evening Post* had found it "a performance in need of immediate sedation, followed by a very long rest."

And poor Tristram, thought Charles wryly, had been through just the same comedic hoops.

But why had he kept the photograph? Sentimentality for his estranged wife? No, Charles had a feeling it was just the eternal actor's ego, which needs bolstering by every reproduction of the subject's image, regardless of the company in which it is taken.

He looked at the other photographs on the page, and found what he was looking for. At the bottom was a posed family group in black and white. It was the Lafeus.

The picture must have been at least fifteen years old. Yves looked younger and was dressed in a conventional suit and tie, but his face still showed a gleam of insolence and mischief. His father stood next to him, face tight with the meanness and self-importance of the bourgeoisie. Beside him Yves's mother looked pale and nervy.

And next to them stood Monique. A slightly gawky girl at the end of her teens, but still unmistakably the ill-tempered pouting woman from Tryst.

Charles took the album downstairs with him, and continued his detailed search in the sitting-room.

On the mantelpiece he found a letter, addressed to "M. Yves Lafeu" at Mas-de-Pouzard. It was postmarked "Reims" and the envelope had been slit open, presumably by some policeman's hand.

Charles took out the sheet inside and read the copybook French of the letter.

My dear son,

I write to confirm that your mother and I will come to stay with you for the week beginning the 20th September. I am writing to Mas-de-Pouzard because the price of postage abroad is so ridiculous.

Your mother has had another attack with her liver recently, and it is important that she has a quiet time.

It will be good to see you after all these years. We only know what we hear from Monique. I wish you would be in touch more. I know your mother would like it, but I understand how expensive postage is, and the telephone is so much it is not worth thinking of it.

Armand Lafeu

"Suppose it was Monique," said Charles.

He was sitting with Bartlemas and O'Rourke round the back of the house, on a terrace overlooking the Lot. They ate slices of rough country pâté with hunks of baguette, and drank the black local wine. The sun was so powerful that they were glad of the shade of the umbrella that rose from the garden table. The setting was so idyllic that talk of murder seemed incongruous.

"You mean suppose she killed Yves?" asked O'Rourke.

"Yes."

"Well, I suppose if she reckoned she would inherit the restaurant, she had a motive."

"Not just the financial one. There was also her deep, deep disapproval of Yves's way of life."

"Yes, but would that have been enough for her to kill him? And why suddenly now?"

"Look at this letter." Charles handed it over. "It looks to me as if Yves's parents knew nothing about his life-style. Monique certainly said she told them nothing about it. So, if they were about to arrive down here to stay with Yves and Tristram, they were in for a bit of a shock."

"And you think she might have killed him to prevent that shock?" asked O'Rourke. In discussion of the murder, Bartlemas seemed content to let his partner do the talking.

"It's possible. Yves might have invited his parents down out of pure mischief and Monique might have killed him to save their feelings."

"So what do you reckon happened?"

"Monique left the restaurant at two, as she said, with the rest of the staff. But my little friend Henry saw a woman going back into the mews round three o'clock. Tristram or Yves would have let her in, of course. Then she killed Yves and forced Tristram to drive the car down here."

"At gunpoint?"

"Presumably."

"Hmm. What, she was hidden in the back of the car?"

"Again—presumably."

"I'm still worried about the risks of going on the boat and—"

"Yes, I agree. That does raise problems. But let's assume that somehow she managed it. They got down here—out of the car— Monique not realizing she's left her lipstick in there. Then she shoots Tristram and hides his body."

"So we're back to finding Tristram's body."

"Yes. Mind you, having seen what the countryside's like round here, I wouldn't give much for our chances. There's the river, lots of cliffs, caves, woods . . ."

"So we're no further advanced? It's still all just speculation."

"Yes, except that if Monique came down here in the Volvo, she must have used some other method of getting back to Reims."

It was at the third car rental agency in Cahors that he struck lucky. Probably he was most lucky in the approach that he took.

"Excuse me," he said in French to the rather plain girl with large glasses who sat behind the desk. "I am trying to trace the movements of a woman."

"Ah. A woman," breathed the girl, infusing the words with deep romance.

"Yes. I'm trying to find where she went, and I believe she may have rented a car from you the Monday before last."

"That was when you last saw her?"

"Well, er—"

"Did you have a bad fight?"

"It wasn't exactly—"

"And now you are full of regrets and wish to find her again," the girl pronounced, not as a question but as a statement. Her fingers were already flicking through a suspended file in her desk drawer.

"Well, yes, that's more or less it," said Charles, seeing no point in disappointing the girl.

"And the woman you are looking for, she is English like you?"

"No, I think French."

"You *think*?"

"French."

The girl extracted a handful of documents from the file. "The Monday, yes. Three cars were rented by women on that day."

"And was one of them called Monique Lafeu?"

"No, Monsieur."

Of course, there was no chance she'd use her real name. Charles produced Tristram's photograph album. "I have a picture of her here. Perhaps . . ."

He opened the book and held it across to the girl.

She looked at the page and gave him a huge smile of complicity. "Yes, Monsieur. That is what she looked like. Yes, your lover did rent a car from us."

Chapter Twelve

EVEN AFTER ONLY a week's break, autumn seemed to have accelerated in England, and Charles felt that he should have worn an overcoat as he walked down from Hereford Road to Tryst.

He wasn't sure yet how to play the scene ahead of him. Monique had sounded frosty on the telephone, but she had not refused to see him. In fact, considering her former manner, she had sounded subdued, as if she was aware of some shift in the balance of power between them, as if she now knew that Charles would be calling the shots.

She sat waiting for him in the stillness of the empty restaurant. Her pout was now less pugnacious, more resigned, and her large body had lost its combative rigidity as she lolled on one of the plush upholstered chairs. The impression that Tryst had been closed down for years was even stronger.

The front door was on the latch and Monique hardly stirred as Charles entered. Inside, he still felt chilly.

"So," said Monique flatly, "you were right."

"Right in some ways. There are still a lot of details to be sorted out."

She looked at him with mild puzzlement. "Right about the restaurant, I meant. Right about the Will. If Yves and Tristram both died, everything was to go to . . . your friend."

"Ah. Yes. Of course, it has not yet been proved that Tristram is dead."

"No." She dismissed this detail with a petulant wave. "So I shouldn't really be here. But I still have the key. And it's somewhere to meet. I did not want you at my apartment."

"So long as the police don't mind you being here."

"They don't seem to mind anything now. They gave me permission to go into the apartment upstairs and sort through Yves's belongings. I think they have lost interest in the case."

"It's the same in France. Though there I don't think they had that much interest in the first place."

"You have been to France?"

"Yes. To Mas-de-Pouzard. I got back yesterday morning."

Monique was silent as she took in this information. Charles waited till she spoke again. "So what do you want from me?"

"I just want to know a little more about the events of the night of your brother's death."

"What?"

"You say you left here at about two?"

"Yes."

"And the next day you went to France?"

"To my parents in Reims, yes. I went by train."

"And after you left the restaurant, you went straight to your flat?"

"Of course."

"You didn't forget anything? You didn't come back to the restaurant for anything?"

"No." She looked sulkier than ever. "Why do you ask?"

"Because I have a witness who saw a woman going into the mews behind here at three o'clock that morning."

"Ah."

"So I'm interested to see if anyone can corroborate that."

There was a pause. "I'm sorry, Mr Paris. I can't help you. As I said, I went straight home."

"I see." Charles changed tack. "Can you think of any reason why anyone would want to kill your brother, Miss Lafeu?"

She shrugged. "In the gay world there is a lot of violence."

"Putting that on one side. Any other reason?"

"No." She hesitated. "Well . . ."

"What?"

"There was something I found. Going through his letters. Just a scrap of paper. It looked like a draft, like a letter he had started and then abandoned."

"What sort of letter?"

"It read like blackmail."

"Do you have the letter?"

"Yes. I found it tucked between the covers of Yves's writing-case."
She reached into her handbag. "Here."

It was just a fragment. The writing was similar to that of Yves's
father. The paper had been torn across the top, and the writing
ended, amid crossings-out, in mid-sentence. What remained was
written in English.

> . . . written them a letter about a chapter from your life-story that
> may have been forgotten. I refer to what happened to Martin
> Sabine, an event that I witnessed. I kept quiet at the time, but now I
> feel they might like to hear about it. The letter will not raise any
> suspicions at this stage, but will show you that I am serious. Of
> course, the right sort of financial offer might make me change my
> mind, but it would have to be . . .

"Yes," said Charles. "It does read like a blackmail letter. There
was nothing else? You've no idea who it was addressed to or . . . ?"
Monique shook her head. "I just found it and thought you might
be interested. After all, it is you who is always looking for 'suspicious
circumstances'."

"Yes."

"Are you finding many?"

"More by the minute."

"And, Mr Paris . . ." Monique leant forward earnestly. "Do any of
these suspicions attach themselves to me?"

"No, Miss Lafeu," said Charles. "None at all."

Tracking down Martin Sabine proved not to be difficult. Charles
knew the name as a fellow-actor, although they had never met.
Spotlight proved unhelpful. Martin had no entry in there, because
most of his work was in radio and voice-overs, but, through a friend
who did a lot of commercials, Charles got the name of an agent. The
agent said that Martin was at the BBC that day doing a radio play.
Charles went at five-thirty to the old Langham Hotel in Portland
Place, where he waited until he saw an actor he knew going into the
BBC Club Bar. He soon met one who was working for the organiz-
ation now known rather poshly as "the BBC Drama Company", but

which Charles still thought of by its old name, "the Rep". This friend obligingly signed Charles in, and at five past six they were each armed with a large Bell's and well-placed to see the arrival of the cast who had been working in the studio all day.

"That's Martin," said the "Rep" actor.

He pointed out a tall, well-built man of about forty, who had his back to them as he approached the bar with a group of other actors. It was only when he came back with his drink and turned his face towards them that Charles knew why Martin Sabine worked mainly in radio and voice-overs.

The actor's face was scored across with old scars, edged with the puckering of stitches. The shape of the face was that of a handsome man, but it was disfigured like something out of a horror film.

The introductions were easily effected, but it took a bit of time and a few drinks before Charles could get Martin on his own and start asking the questions he wanted to.

"Did you know Tristram Gowers and Yves Lafeu?"

"What, the stars of the recent murder mystery?" Martin, when not using one of his remarkable range of professional voices, spoke languidly, slightly effetely. "Hadn't seen them for ages. Tryst wasn't really my scene. But I met them a few times years back."

"Where? Were you in a show with them?"

"No. We were members of the same club." Martin's hand went gently to his face. "A club that I have cause to remember."

"That was where . . . ?"

Martin nodded. "Outside it, yes."

"Do you mind telling me what happened?"

The scarred face made a wry grimace. "Why not? It hardly worries me at all now. I've come to accept it as part of my life. Just one of those things that happened. Divided my life in two. Before, I was poised, as the papers put it, 'on the brink of stardom'. Before, I was even rather beautiful. As beautiful as Yves himself, if you could believe it. Everyone said so. I looked rather like him, too. And now . . ." He shrugged. "Still, I'm very fortunate in having a lot of chums who've stuck by me and, well . . . could be worse."

Charles bided his time, waiting patiently.

"But you want to know what happened. God knows I've told the story enough times, another won't hurt. A face like this really is a conversation-piece. At least it is with the people who dare to mention it. Half of them just gaze appalled, and try to pretend they're ignoring it. Still, on with the story—what there is of it. I'm afraid my narrative is a little slender, but I was unconscious for a good bit of the action.

"Basically, what happened was that I had been in this club we mentioned, round Notting Hill way—it's gone now, been replaced by a video rental shop, but that's by the way. So I had had a pleasant evening, a few drinks, a few dances . . ."

"Do you know if Tristram and Yves were there that night?"

"Quite honestly I can't remember. They could have been. I think it was round that time that Yves started bringing Tristram to the club. They were working on a show quite close to London . . . Bromley or somewhere? I can't remember."

"Sorry to have interrupted."

"Don't worry. So, anyway, I had had a good evening, but I didn't get lucky, so I left the club on my own. Which, as it turned out, was a silly thing to do. The club was set back at the end of an alley, and I'm afraid in that alley, someone was waiting for me—well, perhaps not for me specifically, but I was the one who got the treatment."

"Which was . . . ?"

"I was hit on the head from behind. That pretty well put me out. And when I came to, I found someone had been practising engraving on my face with a broken bottle."

"God."

"Yes, not nice." Martin Sabine sighed. "Still, be thankful for small mercies—at least they didn't touch my eyes."

"So what happened then? Were the police called?"

"Oh, you bet."

"But they didn't catch your attacker?"

"No. But they got me to hospital, and when I was stitched up they came and chatted to me."

"What did they say?"

"Oh, words of infinite comfort. Told me that the attack probably wasn't personal, just—as they charmingly put it—'another case of queer-bashing'. They were sympathetic, but basically they seemed to imply that it was my own fault."

"Your fault?"

"For going to that sort of club, for choosing that sort of company. The old biblical view that 'he that toucheth pitch shall be defiled therewith'."

Charles nodded. It was the same reaction that he had sensed in the police after Yves's death. There had certainly been advances in tolerance of homosexual activity, but much residual prejudice remained.

"And I suppose . . . you didn't get even a glimpse of your attacker?"

Martin laughed, showing his straight, white teeth. The laugh for a moment took attention off his scars, and Charles could see how very good-looking he must once have been.

"If you knew how many times I've been asked that."

"And what answer do you always give?"

"That I didn't see my attacker. That all I got, if anything, was the vaguest of vague impressions."

"And what was that impression?"

Martin laughed again. "Ah, well, this is what makes me realize that one should never trust vague impressions, because they're bound to be misleading."

"Why?"

"Because the impression I got was that my attacker was a woman."

Chapter Thirteen

ZOË FRATTON WAS in when Charles rang the doorbell of her Swiss Cottage flat. He had contemplated telephoning her to check, but had not wished to put her on her guard.

She seemed pleased to see him. She looked better than she had at their previous meeting, her short hair newly trimmed, but there was still the smell of gin on her breath. She replenished her glass when they reached her living-room and provided Charles with a substantial scotch.

"Good to see you, Charles. Got any work?"

He shook his head. "The 'rest' continues."

"Never mind. One day the phone will ring and it'll be Rachel Grant or another of those Casting Directors at the National."

"Oh yes. Of course." Then, knowing he was only putting off the evil moment, he asked, "You got anything coming up?"

"Not a sausage. Beginning to wonder how long I can keep on the flat."

"Something will happen."

"Oh yes," she said with automatic optimism.

They were silent. She looked at him expectantly, and with a sickening feeling Charles realized that she thought he was there because she fancied her. He remembered they had talked idly of sleeping together when they last met. "The day may come . . ." Zoë had said. And perhaps, under other circumstances, he would not have been averse to the idea. But, as things were, it seemed incongruous and tasteless.

He plunged in. "Zoë, I want to talk about Yves's death."

Before she had time to express the surprise that showed in her face, he pressed on. "I want to talk about the night he died. I have a witness who saw who went in and out of the mews that night."

"Ah." Her expression of surprise gave way to one of trapped anxiety.

"A woman was seen entering the mews just before three o'clock. A tall woman."

She looked at him defiantly. "I'm not the only tall woman in the world!"

"No. But I think you were the one who was seen."

She prepared for another defiant reply, but then crumpled. "Oh, why deny it? Who cares? Yes, it was me."

"And what were you intending to do when you went there?"

"It was stupid. Vicious and petty. I just wanted revenge on them. I'd been drinking and was feeling poor and abandoned, and thinking of them about to go off on this wonderful holiday, and I just couldn't stand it. So I planned this petty revenge."

"What did you do?"

"I'll tell you what I planned to do, though, God, when I think about it, I can't believe how small-minded it seems. I just wanted something to disrupt them, to make a mess of their infinitely tidy little lives."

"So . . . ?"

"I bought some meat from my local butcher. Liver. Bought it on the Saturday afternoon. I was drunk. I had this idea that straight after they'd gone away, I'd shove it through their letter-box. Just leave it there for a month, for the flies to get at, so that it would smell and so that when they returned, this vile mess would be there waiting for them. As I say, it sounds pathetic, but I've felt such bitterness towards them."

"What happened when you got to the mews?"

"I saw the lights were still on. I thought they would have already gone, but they hadn't. And suddenly I realized how ridiculously I was behaving, and that doing things like that wouldn't help at all, just make me feel more pathetic than ever. So I left the meat by the door and went home."

It was plausible. Certainly it explained the carrier bag of liver from a Swiss Cottage butcher that Charles had found outside the door of the mews. But, although it dealt with that detail, there were a great many others that it left unexplained.

"I think that may have been your intention, Zoë, and what you have told me may be true. Except for the end. I don't think you went straight home after you had left the meat. In fact, I don't really know why you took the meat. I think, as you said, you were planning revenge. But the revenge you planned was more than a tasteless practical joke. You planned to kill both the man who had taken your husband from you and your husband himself."

Zoë gaped speechless, as Charles went on:

"I think you knocked on the door of the mews and were admitted. I think you killed Yves and then forced Tristram to drive down to the house in France. There you killed him and disposed of his body. Then you rented a car in Cahors and drove back to Calais. You arrived back in England the day when I met you for the first time in the Montrose."

Finally Zoë found speech. "But, Charles, that's ridiculous! Preposterous! It's not true!"

"Zoë, these are the facts. You have never made any secret of how much you hated Yves, and the more time Tristram spent with him, the more you came to hate Tristram too. You were seen entering the mews at three o'clock on the night Yves was murdered. You left a lipstick in Tristram's car. A girl in the car rental agency in Cahors identified you from a photograph. Not only that, the car was rented in your own name. You showed your passport and driving licence as identification. And the car you rented was left for the agency to collect at Calais."

Zoë's head moved from side to side in disbelief. "No, Charles, no. I don't know how you've found all that out, but it's wrong. It just didn't happen. I spent the weekend here."

"Did anyone see you?"

"Well, no . . . I . . . I was drinking. A real bender. I just . . . drank. That's why I was in such a bad state when I saw you at the Montrose."

"It's not the most wonderful alibi in the world, Zoë."

"But it's true. You've got to believe me."

"I wish I could."

"Oh, how can I convince you?" Her despair had that stagey quality that actresses can never quite keep out of their voices.

"Have you got your passport?"

"Yes. I was looking at it recently. Now it should be in this drawer." She moved across to a small bureau.

Charles, who had seen something on top of some books on a shelf, also moved.

"It doesn't seem to be here," said Zoë. When she turned back, Charles was holding her passport. "How on earth did it get there?"

"Do you mind if I look?"

"Go ahead."

He let out a sigh of disappointment.

"What were you hoping to find, Charles?"

"A stamp, a customs stamp. But, of course, they very rarely do stamp them when you're crossing the Channel nowadays."

"No. Charles, I wish I could persuade you how wrong—"

"Ah. Your hairstyle was the same."

"What?"

He held across to her the passport, open at the photograph. It was a younger Zoë, with a page-boy haircut.

"Yes. I had it like that for a show."

"I know."

"*Twelfth Night*. At Bromley."

"Yes. It was from a production photograph of that that the girl in Cahors identified you."

"But how did you—"

"Tristram had kept one. With him as the Clown."

"Oh God . . ." Her voice was now dull and lifeless.

"It was round the time that you got the passport that the marriage broke up, wasn't it?"

"Yes."

"Yves was also in the cast, wasn't he?"

"He was choreographer."

"Yes. It was then that he started flirting with Tristram, that Tristram started getting interested, that the affair started."

Zoë nodded bleakly.

"And it was then that you made your first attack on Yves."

Her head shot up. "What do you mean?"

"What I say."

"We had rows. There were scenes. Not an attack."

Charles's voice remained level as he made the accusation. "I'm talking about the time you waited for Yves outside a gay club in

Notting Hill. The time when you thought you'd slashed his face. The time when you got the wrong person and ruined the career of Martin Sabine."

"Martin Sabine?" she echoed.

"Don't pretend you don't know who I mean."

"I do know who you mean. Radio actor. But I've never met him. Charles, I don't understand. Why are you saying all this?"

"Because I don't believe that people should be allowed to get away with murder."

"But I haven't murdered anyone, Charles." She was weeping now, huge tears of frustration or disbelief. "Really. I haven't. I couldn't."

"There's a lot of evidence against you, Zoë. The girl in Cahors identified you immediately."

Zoë Fratton went suddenly limp. All resistance seemed to have drained out of her. "What do you propose to do, Charles?"

"I think we go to the police."

"And   ?"

"And you confess."

"Yes. Why not?" she asked with sudden recklessness. "That really would be the ultimate irony of my career, wouldn't it? At least someone would be giving me the chance to play a big scene for once. Oh, God, that show in Bromley. Everything was all right until that show in Bromley. I was really set to go places. Playing Viola—huh, next stop the West End. And then it all started to crumble. Tristram . . . that's when I started drinking heavily. That's when it all fell apart."

"I'm sorry, Zoë. Perhaps I ought to phone the police."

"Oh yes," she said cynically. "At least you don't have to pay rent in prison. And it's a good excuse for not having a job."

"Yes," said Charles gently, and moved across to the telephone.

"It was a good production, though, the *Twelfth Night*. Press loved it. Even talk of a transfer at one stage, though of course that was nonsense—RSC's got the West End sewn up so far as Shakespeare's concerned. But we got some good notices. First time some of the critics had understood Orsino's love-sickness, first time Malvolio had taken on genuine tragic stature, first time the twins had actually looked like twins—all that kind of stuff. Oh, only local press, I know, but you can't help believing that sort of praise, at least at the time. I was the great new discovery—after twelve years in the business I was finally being discovered. And what did it lead to? Nothing. Nothing for any of us. Huh, the only one who went anywhere after that show was my dear brother."

"Brother?"

"Twin. Sebastian. You know, 'One face, one voice, one habit, and two persons . . .'"

Charles continued Orsino's speech automatically. "'A natural perspective, that is, and is not!'"

"That's the one."

"And who played Sebastian?"

"Bertram Pride."

"Oh, my God," said Charles Paris.

Chapter Fourteen

DANA WILSON'S VOICE sounded as languorous and put-upon as ever. To those who have nothing to do, even the smallest demand on their time becomes an imposition.

"It's Charles Paris."

"Who?"

"An actor. We met the Friday before last."

"Oh." She sounded doubtful of his claim.

"We were introduced through my agent."

"Oh, Marcus Scrotton, yes. I remember."

It was near enough. Charles didn't bother to correct her. But so much for your photographic memory, he thought. A chap could die locked away in your mind and you'd never notice.

"I'm afraid nothing's come up," said Dana. "And I'd really rather you didn't ring me. As soon as there is anything suitable I will be in touch with your agent."

"Yes, it wasn't work that I was ringing about."

"Oh." This was a monosyllable of pure surprise. What else could an actor be ringing about? She followed it with another "Oh", this one registering mild interest.

"No. If I remember rightly, you said that you cast *Lexton and Sons.*"

"Oh yes," she replied in a new tone of gratification. "Well, when I saw the first scripts I just knew their faces instinctively. I knew that Millicent had to be Rita Lexton, and of course George was born to play—"

"Yes." Charles cut into the orgy of self-congratulation. "It's the part of Philip I'm interested in."

"Well, that was Bertram Pride. I thought everyone knew that—"

"I know Bertram Pride actually *played* the part, but I thought you said he wasn't your first choice."

"Well, we had a lot of interviews for the part. A lot of actors were considered. In the end we cut them down to two."

"Bertram Pride and your first choice?"

"Yes. An actor called Martin Sabine. Don't know if you know him. Does mostly radio now."

"I know him." Charles's voice was thick with relief.

"Well, it had been decided that he should play the part. Very clever actor he was. And extraordinarily good-looking."

Her emphasis on the last words made Charles reflect that she would have been barking up the wrong tree if she had hoped for a little dalliance with Martin as one of the perks of her profession.

"But then he had this terrible accident. Don't know if you heard—he was beaten up. Horrible. And I'm afraid he looked such a mess afterwards, there was no way he could be Philip. Thank God it happened before the contracts had actually been signed or before any publicity had gone out." Then, in case that sounded too callous, she added, "I mean, the company did make him some sort of *ex gratia* payment, though they weren't under any obligation to do so."

"So you went ahead with Bertram?"

"Yes. And he was frightfully good. Another of my little moments of inspiration. And did you know that I discovered Wally Gammons . . . and Frank Stillman . . . and—"

"Thank you," said Charles, and rang off.

"So you reckon," asked Zoë, "that Bertram took my passport when he came round the few days before Yves died."

Charles nodded. "I would think so. Did the subject of passports come up?"

"It did, actually. He started talking about publicity photographs and saying how impossible it was to get a good likeness. Then he got on to passport photographs and asked to see mine. I hadn't had my passport out for ages. Took me some time to find it. But I did. And he must have just palmed it."

"You'd had a few drinks, hadn't you?" She nodded. "So you probably weren't watching him too closely."

"And I thought," she said bitterly, "he'd just come round out of friendship, just brought me the gin for old times' sake."

"I'm rather afraid the gin was part of his plan."

"What, you mean he knew I was likely to go on a bender and . . ."

"Set yourself up with a lost weekend, yes."

"Oh God. Is that the reputation I've got now? I really will give it up, you know. I really will stop."

"Yes," he said soothingly. "I often say that."

"And then Bertram must have put the passport back the next week when he turned up with another bottle of gin. I can't actually see why he bothered about that. I'd never have noticed the passport was gone for ages, and he was just drawing attention to the connection between us."

"Ah, but you forget. You got the possibility of that job on the feature film in Tunisia. You told Bertram about it when he rang you on the Wednesday morning. Must've given him a nasty shock. If you'd got it, you would suddenly have needed your passport in a hurry."

"So he came round full of more gin and sympathy and deposited it on my bookshelves."

"Where I found it, yes."

"My God. The sod. He'd got it all worked out. But why?"

"Because of the blackmail. Yves had been at the club the night Martin Sabine was attacked. He saw what happened."

"And you mean Bertram was dressed as me that night too?"

"He was wearing the wig he wore in *Twelfth Night*, and he was dressed in women's clothes. On that occasion his aim wasn't to look like you, just not to look like himself. But that must have been what gave him the idea for the later crime."

"But Yves saw the attack on Martin?"

"That's what this letter says." Charles produced the sheet that Monique had given him.

"Can you prove any of this, Charles?"

He shook his head lugubriously. "Not yet. I haven't got any solid proof. But this time I'm convinced I'm right."

"You sounded pretty convinced you were right when you were accusing me of everything under the sun," Zoë chided him gently.

"No, but this time . . ." He grinned and stopped himself. "I will prove it. There's something in this blackmail letter. I'm assuming the final draft was sent to Bertram, but it also refers to Yves's having 'written them a letter about a chapter from your life-story that may have been forgotten'."

"And who do you think 'them' is? The police?"

"No," said Charles. "Not the police."

He decided that a journalistic approach was best. Showman Books seemed to be a company whose success was based solely on immediate publicity, and he reckoned the Editorial Director would be likely to give an interview to anyone who promised him more of the same. His guess proved correct.

Showman Books produced paperback originals about show business. They were brought out quickly, in large quantities, in the wake of any established media success and, for a very short period, they sold well. Much of the list was "stories of the making of" various films and television series. It also included quiz-books, cook-books and gardening books compiled by hacks and sold under the name of the star whose face beamed from the front cover. And, of course, they sold autobiographies, ghosted autobiographies, picture biographies and "as told to" life-stories of all the flavour-of-the-month stars. These had titles like *On A Green Light, Mr Thwaite, We'll Have To Lose the Hippo*, and *Not In These Knickers I Won't*: they got serialized in the less serious newspapers, were the subject of many plugging media interviews, and sold in their thousands during their bursts of publicity.

The operation of Showman Books was, as a director of an older-established, more conventional and less financially stable publishing house put it, "media-mushroom-farming".

Charles had selected his journalist's voice with care. He decided that he would do better to claim to represent a foreign publication, as this meant that his credentials were less likely to be checked. He thought of being American, Hank Bergheimer perhaps, European Correspondent of the *Pennsylvania Falls Gazette-Tribune* or something. Then he could use the voice he'd had in *The Front Page* ("Until last night I didn't think this play *could* drag"—*Leicester Mercury*). But he concluded that that might sound a bit "over the top" after more than five minutes and so settled for the Australian twang he had developed for what the play's author had described as "a *commedia del arte* interpretation of the Ned Kelly story" ("The knowledge that Arts Council money helped to put on this production is enough to make any taxpayer's blood boil"—*Romford Recorder*). Somehow the Australian voice suited the crassly insensitive style of questioning that Charles was planning.

When he rang through to fix the interview Charles hit his first snag. Not that the Editorial Director was unwilling to talk. No, according to his secretary, Frank Clayton would be delighted to give up half an hour to the *Perth Examiner*. The catch came in the next sentence, "He's always happy to do a favour to a fellow-Aussie."

Still, the interview was set up and Charles didn't want to risk losing it by starting again in another persona. Great, he would look forward to meeting Mr Clayton at four-thirty that afternoon.

Showman Books' editorial offices were two floors over a dubbing theatre in Berwick Street. As Charles entered the building, he felt anxious. It wasn't the first time that he had chosen the wrong accent and been confronted with one of its native speakers. And he knew the situation could become awkward. He tried hastily to fabricate a background for Bill Bunyan, his chosen name, which would explain how far away he had come from his roots.

The offices were small and untidy. Manuscripts and books were piled everywhere; on the walls old jacket proofs, artwork and signed stars' publicity photographs were pinned haphazardly. The visible staff of Showman Books appeared to be two harassed girls, busy over typewriters in the outer office, and Frank Clayton himself, an oversize man in shirtsleeves with a little beard like a paintbrush stuck on the point of his chin.

Clayton greeted him effusively. "Always great to see another exile, sport. You just come over for a trip, have you?"

"No, I'm based in Europe. Paris. Seventeen years since I was actually in the old country."

"Yes, I've been based here over twenty, but I get back most winters—that is, winter here, I hasten to add, summer back home. I still got family out there. You say you're on the *Perth Examiner*?"

"That's right."

"Perth where you come from?"

"Yes," said Charles, taking a chance.

"Oh, I'm from Brisbane."

Charles heaved a sigh of relief. He had hoped that by choosing

Perth as a birthplace and Paris as a base he would avoid embarrassing questions about mutual friends or well-loved places, and the gamble appeared to have paid off. And, so far, Frank Clayton was showing no suspicion of the accent.

"Was it anything specific that you wanted to ask me about, Bill?"

Charles lied. "No, just general publication plans. Any big titles you got coming up, that sort of thing."

"Yes, well, we've got some goodies coming for Christmas, let me tell you. So those'll mostly be published in Australia say six months hence. When were you planning to do your piece for the paper?"

"I have a fairly flexible brief. And obviously, if there's anything where we can tie in publication with a television series re-run back home, then all to the good."

"Now you're talking," said Clayton, going in exactly the direction that Charles wanted to push him. "You know that *Lexton and Sons* is as big in Australia as it is here—even bigger, I reckon. Well, they're supposed to be running the last series on Channel 9—you never know with television scheduling, they keep changing it—but we've got a book coming that's really going to sell, if it ties in with that. You know Bertram Pride, who plays Philip?"

Charles nodded.

"Well, we're doing a very nice autobiography with him. Good story. All the 'How I Became An Overnight Success' bit. And the heartache too . . . you know, times out of work—even a big star like him had his patches of 'resting'. Then there's the marriage, break-up of the marriage, girl-friends—you know, he's had affairs with some really good names. It's all in there. Really going to sell, that book. It's called *A Pride of Lextons*. Not bad, eh? Like a Pride of Lions, you know. Gets his name and the series name in the title. No, that book's really going to move in the best-seller lists."

"That's great," said Charles. "Just the sort of thing I need for my article. Was it a difficult book to get together?"

"No, not really. Well, WET wanted a ridiculous amount for the use of stills from the series—they don't seem to realize that it's free publicity for them. But we sorted that out. Had to give them an arm and a leg, but it got settled. Bertram himself was easy. Charming fellow, you know."

Bill Bunyan agreed with this opinion. Charles Paris didn't.

"As a matter of fact, Frank, I did meet Bertram recently at a party and he was talking about the book. That's really why I wanted to see you. I mean, interested in the other titles as well, of course, but *A Pride of Lextons* sounds to be the big one."

"Say that again. Comes out in two weeks here. Just peak for Christmas. Have you had a copy yet?"

Charles shook his head. Frank Clayton reached round to a shelf behind him and handed one over. The cover was a close-up of Bertram. The lettering of the title covered his hair, and all Charles was aware of was how strikingly like Zoë Fratton's the bone-structure was. He felt sure that this time he was on the right track.

This certainty gave him courage and inspiration for his next line of questioning. "When I met Bertram, he said you were getting a lot of media interest in the book."

"Too right. He'll be doing Wogan, *Start the Week*, *Pebble Mill*, signings, the whole works."

"He also said you'd even had letters about the book before publication . . ."

"What?" Frank Clayton looked puzzled, and Charles feared that he had taken a wrong turning and wouldn't get the information he required.

"Bertram said you'd had letters from fans about the book," he amplified hopefully.

"Oh yes, one or two, certainly," said Clayton, and Charles breathed again.

"He was very encouraged by that, said it was unusual, promised well for the book . . ."

"Certainly does."

"And he said I should ask you to let me see the letters, just to show how the whole thing was building up . . ."

"Oh."

Charles pressed home his advantage. "I want to get as full a background for my article as possible. I mean, when it's syndicated all over Australia, that's going to be a good few potential book-buyers who—"

"Yes, yes, of course," said Frank Clayton, and reached up for a file behind him.

There were half a dozen letters looking forward to the publication of *A Pride of Lextons*. They all appeared to be from gushing middle-aged housewives, the backbone of Philip Lexton's fans.

But one of them was in handwriting that Charles Paris recognized.

"I wonder . . . would it be possible to have copies of these? It's just, you know, a different angle on the celebrity bit . . . And, of course, would bring in a little more about the publisher. You know, mention the name of Showman Books a few more times . . ."

One of the harassed-looking girls was summoned to take photocopies.

To maintain his alias, Charles then had to listen to three-quarters of an hour on the amazing sales potential of *Christopher Milton's Guide for Gormless Gardeners*, *The Bernard Walton Book of Car Games for Kids* and George Birkitt's no-punches-pulled autobiography, *No Llamas in the Dressing-Room*.

But he didn't mind. He had got what he had come for. The writing on the letter was the same as that on the paper which Monique had given him. The text was short.

Dear Mr Clayton,

    I can't wait to get hold of a copy of Bertram Pride's book. I have followed his career closely right from the start and am longing to read all the details, particularly of his work with Martin Sabine. I am sure the press are going to be interested in the whole story. Lots of luck with the book.

                         Yours faithfully,
                         Eve Fire (Mrs)

To Frank Clayton it was just another letter, an effusion from one of Bertram's blue-rinsed fans who perhaps hadn't got her facts right.

But to Bertram Pride it must have been something very different. Its message was unambiguous. The apparently irrelevant mention of Martin Sabine was loaded with meaning, and the transparent pseudonym, so typical of Yves's mischievous method, left no room for doubt.

Perhaps Bertram had been unworried by the letter that Yves had sent to him. Perhaps he thought he could charm his way out of it. But when Yves started writing to his publisher, it was clear that the threat was genuine. Yves really would expose the criminal origins of Bertram Pride's "overnight success".

Which meant, so far as the star of *Lexton and Sons* was concerned, that Yves Lafeu had to be killed.

Chapter Fifteen

"I DON'T KNOW whether Mel'd wear it, Charles. He's got a business to run, and if he starts doing that sort of thing, well, if it gets around, he could lose a lot of contraceptive."

"Translate, Stan," said Charles, resigned.

"Contraceptive pill—Goodwill."

"You do make them up."

"Never."

They were sitting in Stan's "little Charlie" (Charlie Chan—van—remember?) outside the Hereford Road house.

"Look, I've got to get inside Bertram Pride's flat and I can't see any other way of doing it. We know Mel supplies cleaners for him, so he must have a key."

"Yeah, but the whole basis of a domestic agency is that it's, like, secure. No one's going to get stuff nicked or anything. Once Mel starts letting people in to his client's gaffs, well, he ceases to be reliable, dunnee?"

"Stan, this is really important."

"Why?"

"It's to do with Yves's murder."

"Oh yes. How?"

"I'll tell you. But, Stan, you must swear not to tell a soul, because the kind of allegations I'm making are certainly slanderous until I've got some more proof."

"You can trust me, Charlie. I'll be as quiet as the permanent."

Permanent wave—Grave. It had to be.

So Charles went through his complete reconstruction of the case, of all Bertram Pride's crimes from the sabotage of Martin Sabine, which had given him the part of Philip Lexton, right up to the presumed murder of Tristram Gowers at Mas-de-Pouzard.

"Hmm," Stan grunted after a long pause. "And none of it can be proved until Tristram's body's found in France."

"Perhaps not even then. The whole plan depended on making that death look like suicide. I'm sure if his body is found it'll be with a gunshot wound through his mouth or at the bottom of the Lot with a stone tied round his neck."

Stan grunted again. "But the French cops are looking for him?"

"Without great enthusiasm. It's difficult country to search there. Bartlemas, O'Rourke and I tried a day's driving round and looking, but there are so many thousands of places where a body could be hidden. I suppose he will be found eventually. Probably not as a result of a search, just dug up by wild animals, found by picnickers, you know, the usual story."

Stan nodded slowly. "There's one bit I don't get, though. Bertram came back from Cahors or whatever you said, disguised as Zoë . . ."

"On her passport, yes."

"Did he go down disguised as her, an' all?"

"I suppose he must have done. Certainly if he went through customs, he did. If he was hidden in the back of the Volvo, perhaps he didn't."

"Hmm. That's the bit that seems odd. I mean, Tristram driving all that way with Bertram keeping a gun on him all the time. You'd have thought Tristram could have got away. Bertram must have got out to do a pee or something, you'd think Tristram'd just have driven off."

"Well, obviously he didn't."

"No." Stan didn't sound totally convinced. "Bloody elaborate crime."

"Yes. But if it had worked, it would have been perfect. It would have got rid of Yves and provided an explanation of his murder. And you forget, the body was discovered so much earlier than had been intended. If we hadn't been doing the decorating, it would have been a month after the murder and most of the trails would have gone cold."

"Seem to have gone pretty cold as it is. Still, as you say, no bloody proof."

"No. Which is all the more reason why I need to get inside Bernard's flat."

"Yeah. We'll go and see Mel."

And Stan turned the key in the ignition of his "Charlie".

An hour later he emerged from the door of Mel Ponting's Fulham Road office, jauntily swinging a key-ring from his little finger, and came towards Charles waiting in the van.

"Right, we're on. Tomorrow morning."

"What did you tell him?"

"Nothing, really. Just that we needed to do it. He wasn't keen, but he owes me an electric."

"Electric tea urn—Good turn?" suggested Charles hopefully.

"No, you great berk. Electric shaver—Favour."

"Oh."

"Mel was very reasonable about it. Only conditions he made—it's got to be both of us goes in . . . and if anything gets broken or goes missing, he'll string us up by our balls from the nearest light-fitting."

"Sounds fair enough."

"Like I say, reasonable man, Mel. He also said there could be some real charring coming up for you in the not-too-distant."

"Good."

"And he's been recommending us round like mad on the old decorating."

"Excellent. The money scene doesn't get any better."

"No. He says the cleaner goes into the flat at nine, and Bertram's usually out at some health club or something. He's not usually back till after the cleaner finishes at twelve."

"I don't think the search'll take anything like three hours."

"Ah, that was another of Mel's conditions."

"What?"

"We do actually have to clean the bloody flat."

Bertram Pride's flat in Hans Place was like the set for a coffee commercial. It was so neat, so consciously "designed" as to be completely without character. There seemed no necessity to clean its immaculate surfaces.

The setting reflected the man. Charles had observed that many actors who became successful took on the trappings of their new wealth like a new set of stage props, objects with which they could work convincingly, with which they could appear at ease, but which did not ultimately belong to them. Many of the most skilful actors, who can slip with facility into other characters like well-tailored suits, have but the sketchiest sense of their own identity. It is this quality that is their strength, that gives them the ability to be more real onstage than in their daily lives. It was also this quality, Charles reflected, that had enabled Bertram to think himself into the role of Zoë Fratton, to dress like her, to walk like her, during the time of his necessity to *become* her.

In spite of the flat's immaculate appearance, Stan insisted that they should keep Mel Ponting's condition and actually clean it. Grudgingly, he agreed that he should do the work, while Charles made his search.

"Though I wish I knew what you was looking for, Charlie," he said as he donned a flowered apron and extracted the Hoover from a cupboard.

"So do I," said Charles. "I just can't think of anywhere else to look. I'm sure I'm going to find something."

He looked across at Stan, who had now donned a flowered headscarf as well, and giggled.

"Now watch it!" Stan shook a finger at him. "And listen, if you ever tell my missus about this, I'll bloody murder you."

"Why?"

"Our marriage is based on her belief that I have a physiological incapacity to do housework. If she ever found out I'd been seen Hoovering I'd never have no peace no more."

Charles searched methodically. Any search where you don't know what you're looking for is difficult, but at least in this case the anonymous neatness of the flat left few corners where secrets could lie undiscovered.

While Stan Hoovered, dusted and polished with a delicacy surprising in one so large, Charles went through the drawers and bookshelves of the living-room. The only item he found that had any relevance to his quest was a new Michelin road map, Number 79, which covered the area round Cahors. And, though that gratifyingly fed his suspicions, in no way could it have been regarded as evidence of any misdoing.

He moved to the small hall and searched its one coat-cupboard, but that revealed nothing untoward. The contents of the bathroom and kitchen were equally predictable and unhelpful.

While Stan whistled cheerfully as he scrubbed the kitchen floor, Charles progressed to the bedroom. This again was out of television-commercial-land, a splendid room with exclusive Knightsbridge views, dominated by a huge suede-covered double bed set into the wall between two fitted cupboards.

The dressing-table yielded nothing.

The right-hand wardrobe revealed only the very extensive selection of clothes required by the suave celebrity-about-town. The pockets of all of the suits and trousers had been meticulously emptied. Serried rows of shirts rose, crisply packaged from the laundry. Underwear, socks and shoes were arranged with the same punctiliousness. Again Charles had the impression of emptiness, of a void where the owner's character should be.

It was the second cupboard that proved interesting.

Its contents were all women's clothes. Most of them were dressing-gowns and night-dresses. Presumably, since it was some time since Bertram had had a live-in girl-friend, these were just part of the professional seducer's kit, comforts to be offered to Rent-A-Totties who unexpectedly stayed overnight, just like something out of the movies.

But it was the day-clothes that interested Charles. Perhaps they had been left by the last girl who had been more than a one-night stand, but that did not conform with the obsessive tidiness of the rest of the flat. Surely, as soon as the woman had gone, someone like Bertram would remove all traces of her.

Also, Charles realized as he pulled out the hangers and looked at them, the clothes were remarkably large.

About Zoë Fratton's size.

About Bertram Pride's size.

He examined the suits and dresses for . . . what? Bloodstains?

There was nothing. All had recently been cleaned. They still bore the labels and wore their polythene shrouds. If they ever had showed evidence of murder, all such traces had been removed.

In the corner of the cupboard was a pile of light brown boxes.

Charles recognized them instantly; he had had enough false hair from Wig Creations in his time to know them at a glance.

With mounting excitement, he reached towards the top box. It contained a blond wig and matching beard.

The second held a similar set in black.

The others contained more, in a variety of hair colours.

Charles knew that the very famous often resorted to disguise when they wished to go out unnoticed. Bertram Pride's television face would have ensured constant interruptions to his social life by ill-disguised stares and requests for autographs. And, though often he might have revelled in these attentions, there must have been times when he sought anonymity and found it through this selection of camouflage.

Charles reached for the bottom box and opened it.

A warm glow filled and relaxed him. He had been right, after all. Now he had evidence.

What was more, he could now explain every detail of Bertram Pride's crime.

Gingerly, he picked the wig out of its nest of tissue paper and held it on his upturned hand. It was beautifully made, a page-boy cut exactly reproducing the one Zoë had worn in *Twelfth Night*. Yes, Viola and Sebastian must have looked identical—no wonder the critics had commented on the fact.

And this hairstyle, too, was exactly the one that appeared in the photograph in Zoë Fratton's passport.

He reached into the tissue paper for the second item. The more important item.

It was a moustache. A grey, gauze-backed walrus moustache. Exactly like that worn by Tristram Gowers.

Charles walked into the sitting-room, holding one of his trophies in each hand. Stan heard him and came in from the kitchen.

"Got something?"

"And how," said Charles.

At that moment they heard the key in the front-door lock, and Bertram Pride walked in. He was wearing a smartly-cut pale

164

grey track-suit, and still glowed from his exercise at the health club.

He took in Stan in his apron and headscarf first. "Ah, you're new," he said amiably, extending a hand. "I'm Bertram Pride."

Then he saw Charles. And what Charles was carrying.

"What the hell are you doing?"

"I'm holding your disguises, Bertram." He raised one hand. "The wig you wore when you came back from Cahors as Zoë Fratton." He raised the other hand. "And the moustache you wore, together with his toupé and glasses, when you drove down to Mas-de-Pouzard, disguised as Tristram Gowers!"

Bertram Pride said nothing. He just turned and rushed out of the flat.

Stan and Charles felt the room shake as the door slammed.

Chapter Sixteen

"SHALL I GO after him?" asked Stan, stripping off his flowered apron.

"No point in chasing him from here," said Charles. "We'll meet him at his destination."

"But how do you know where he's going to be?"

"I think there's a strong chance he'll be with Tristram Gowers' body."

"What, down in bleeding France?"

"No. That's the whole point. I've been trying desperately to work out where the second person went in the Volvo, and all the time I should only have been thinking of one person. Tristram Gowers was an easy person to impersonate. His face was all props rather than features. Anyone with brown eyes who was tall enough could put on a false moustache and, with the wig and glasses, he'd pass—certainly well enough for a busy official comparing a passport photograph."

"So you mean he drove down to the house in France dressed as Tristram and came back as Zoë?"

"Exactly."

"But you don't think Tristram's still alive?"

Charles shook his head. "I'm afraid not. But it's no wonder the French police had no luck finding his body, since the body never even went to France. And the English police, who might have found it here, had no reason to start looking."

"So where do you reckon it is?"

Charles was already dialling on the telephone as he answered. "I have only one idea. If I'm wrong, we're virtually back to square one. But, thinking about it, on the night Bertram killed Yves and Tristram, he didn't have much time. He left the mews at half past three, and he caught the six-thirty ferry at Dover. He couldn't afford a major detour and he couldn't risk just dumping the body. He had to put it somewhere safe and then probably move it to a final resting-place once interest in the case had died down."

166

"But where would—"

Finally the telephone was answered at the other end.

"Henry," said Charles, interrupting Stan.

"Sorry, I was in the bath," her Kensington vowels replied.

"Listen, Henry, this is important. You remember the great dirty weekend which didn't take place . . . ?"

"With Bertram? Yes." Her voice sounded small.

"Don't feel bad about it. You were set up, I'm afraid. He planned to fix the weekend and then stage a row with you so that it didn't happen."

"But I don't see what—"

"I can't explain now. Tell me, did you ever find out the address of his cottage in Kent?"

When he was in a hurry, Stan Fogden's style of driving the "Charlie" was hair-raising. After a particularly spine-jarring corner, Charles remonstrated, "Hey, look, nothing's going to be gained if we don't get there in one piece."

"Don't worry, mate. I know what I'm doing. Every other telly I get I'm driving the getaway jam-jar. I done more drives like this than you've had hot saintsands."

Saints and sinners—Dinners, Charles translated for himself, as he clung grimly to the door-handle of the van and prayed that his idea about Bertram's movements was correct.

The address Henry had given was in a little village outside Canterbury. Going there would have involved only the smallest detour on the route from London to Dover, and that fact fuelled the hope in Charles's mind.

As they approached the cottage and saw its remoteness from the village of its postal address, Charles also felt hope. It was an ideal place for a temporary morgue. If the cottage had a cellar . . . or an outhouse . . . Even a temporary grave in the garden might be possible. You don't have to be over-elaborate in your concealment of a body when the search for it is centred in another country.

Stan parked just to the side of the closed gate. The cottage, like all the accoutrements of Bertram Pride's life, had the heightened reality

167

of a commercial. Its thatch was too neat, its beams too black, its paintwork too white.

There appeared to be no sign of life. The garage door, like the front gate, was closed. There was no car in evidence.

"I hope to God we aren't too late," Charles muttered. "If he's off hiding the body somewhere really secure, bang goes our evidence."

"Assuming of course," said Stan cheerfully, "that it ever was here in the first place . . ."

"Thank *you*," said Charles. "Wait in the van. I'll just go and have a snoop around."

"Sure you don't want me to come? Like I say, I have played a few heavies in my time."

"No, you watch the gate, in case he tries to get out this way. And if I'm not back in half an hour, get the police."

"Yeah," said Stan ruefully. "That's the line that always gets said to me in tellies. Means I've had my little scene and now the camera's going to follow the bleeding 'ero into the bleeding 'ouse."

Charles grinned and got out of the van. He tapped it on the roof, glad of Stan's presence, as he moved towards the gate.

There were tyre-marks on the gravel and an arc scraped by the opening gate, but he could not tell how recently the marks had been made. As he clicked the latch and pushed the gate, he felt an awful emptiness. If Bertram Pride wasn't there, if Bertram Pride had not been there that day, then Charles's whole theory was wrong.

Although the cottage itself was fairly small, it was set fifty yards back from the road, so the drive was long. Charles moved forward slowly. Over the garage door he could see a video camera fixed, trained on the gate. Another of the celebrity props, a way of vetting visitors, no doubt keeping away the fans.

Though the camera was trained on him, Charles got no feeling of being watched. The emptiness within him grew more hollow.

What happened happened very suddenly.

Remotely controlled, the garage door slid up and over.

The Range Rover inside must have been already started and revving, because it leapt forward like a race-horse out of the stalls.

Charles just had time to register Bertram Pride's face, expressionless, behind the windscreen, as the car rushed, in a fusillade of gravel, towards him.

He urged his body to the side, but, as in a dream of running in sand, it responded with agonizing slowness.

The Range Rover's bumper caught him on the hip, lifting him, spinning him like a child's toy before throwing him down in a flower-bed.

Winded as he lay there, Charles turned his head to the car's back, and saw it disappearing through the gate which he had so obligingly left open. Bertram Pride had got away.

But Charles had reckoned without Stan Fogden. There was a sudden screech and earth-shaking impact as the little "Charlie" was driven into the Range Rover's path.

Bertram Pride was out of his vehicle first. Stan's driving-side door was smashed in and he had to get out the other side. As Charles hobbled up to the gate, Bertram had set off down the lane, with Stan a good ten yards behind.

But, despite his bulk, and despite Bertram's fitness programme, Stan moved the faster. He launched himself into an untidy tackle which brought Bertram crashing down on to the tarmac.

Stan was first up. And, as Bertram rose, a fist with some eighteen stones' weight behind it caught him neatly on the point of the jaw. Like a figure from a *Tom and Jerry* cartoon, his body stiffened and he went back down on to the road like a board.

"Bit of rope in the back of the van," Stan shouted to Charles. "Bring it along. We'll truss him up."

As Charles approached, Stan was flexing and unflexing his right hand with evident pain.

"Cor blimey. I've swung that punch in so many tellies, but I'm used to the bloke ducking back before I hit him. Bloody hurts when you actually make contact."

Bertram groaned as his arms and legs were pinioned, but he was out to the world.

"That was quite amazing, Stan, the way you stopped the car and caught him. It was like something out of *The Sweeney*."

The fat actor shrugged. "First time I done it *was* actually on a *Sweeney*. But I've played the scene in a good few other tellies too.

Shows the benefit of rehearsal, Charles my old son. Had to get this right first time. 'Cause there's no retakes in real have-you-met-the, is there?"

The context gave that one away. Have-you-met-the-wife?—Life.

Their next task was grimmer.

Charles opened the Range Rover's hatchback.

The smell that came from the huge sealed black polythene bag was not too strong. But when they cut the adhesive tape that held it, the stench suddenly flooded up like gas, invading their mouths and nostrils.

Gagging, they stayed only long enough to confirm that the bag did contain a corpse, and then called the police.

The latter's investigations confirmed that the bag contained, as well as a bloody razor and bloodstained gloves and clothes, the body of Tristram Gowers.

Although after so long it was difficult to fix the precise time of death, it seemed likely that he had been strangled the night Tryst had been closed for its annual holiday.

Charles only hoped that Tristram had died before he saw what Bertram did to his lover.

Chapter Seventeen

"HE WAS AMBITIOUS," said Charles. "He had been out of work, and he was determined it wasn't going to happen again. Martin Sabine stood between him and that part, and he was determined to get it. That was where Bertram went wrong. If he hadn't attacked Martin, he wouldn't have needed to commit the other two murders."

"He very nearly got away with them . . ." said O'Rourke.

"Very nearly . . ." Bartlemas agreed.

They were sitting over one of Bartlemas's "divine" French meals, drinking the black wine of Cahors. The face that might have been Edmund Kean as Sir Giles Overreach beamed malevolently down on them.

"I wonder why Yves waited so long before he started blackmailing Bertram . . . ?"

"I don't know," said Charles. "Sheer mischief, perhaps. Perhaps he needed money for his other activities, for conducting the affairs Tristram wasn't meant to know about."

"It's quite possible . . ."

"He was a very naughty boy . . ."

"But he did love Tristram . . ."

"Oh yes, in his way he loved him . . ."

"And presumably," said Charles, "just paying Yves off was too risky. So long as Yves was alive, there would be the constant danger of exposure. And if Tristram knew about the attack too . . ."

"Do you think he did?"

"There was a risk that he might. Also Bertram's plan depended on an absent Tristram on whom Yves's death could be blamed."

"Yes. Poor Tris . . ."

"Poor dear Tris . . ."

"Bertram planned it for a long time. He set up Gary Stane, using a French accent to throw suspicion on to Yves. He set up poor little Henry, planning the row with her all the time."

"Cynical . . ."

"And cold-blooded . . ."

"Yes. But, you know, he was at a very dangerous time in his career."

"Oh, surely not . . ."

"*Lexton and Sons* had made him a star, surely . . ."

"Yes, but the last series of *Lexton and Sons* was over. There was still money coming in—foreign repeats, that sort of thing—but Bertram had a very high standard of living to maintain. He was 'resting' too, you know—had been since the last series finished. And it's much more difficult for a 'star'—he has to select what he does with great care, wait for the right property. That's why the book was so important to him. *A Pride of Lextons*, with all its attendant promotion, was going to bring Bertram Pride back into the public eye, remind them that he was a star."

"Hmm. I suppose the book will be withdrawn . . ."

"Pulped, I expect . . ."

"Having met its publisher, I wouldn't be surprised if he doubled the print order. All this is going to give him more free publicity than he ever dreamed of."

There was a silence. Bartlemas served their *digestif*, brandy-soaked prunes from Agen, part of the loot from the French trip.

"Are you going to have these on the menu in Tryst when you take it over, O'Rourke?" asked Charles.

"Not a bad idea . . ."

"O'Rourke talked to the solicitors today . . ."

"Yes, it's confirmed . . ."

"He does get the lot . . ."

"And are you going to keep it on?"

"I had a rather bizarre idea about that." O'Rourke smoothed his residue of hair across his scalp. "I thought I'd get Monique Lafeu in to manage it."

"She seemed to be a pretty tough businesswoman."

"Exactly. No great sense of humour, but she'd run it well. In a strange way, I feel that Yves might have approved . . ."

"I think you're right, O'Rourke . . ."

"I'm also going to make over some of the money to Zoë. God

172

knows, we don't need it, and she got a very rough deal out of the divorce . . ."

"Very rough . . ." Bartlemas echoed.

"That's an extremely kind thought," said Charles. "And it'd really be appreciated. She's desperately hard-up. Mind you, you'd better put a condition to the gift."

"What?"

"That she's not allowed to spend any of it on gin."

Bartlemas and O'Rourke shook their heads sadly.

"Heard she was going a bit that way . . ."

"Such a pity . . . Lovely girl . . ."

"Yes. All she needs is a few good jobs. If she had the work, she wouldn't feel the need to drink."

"No . . ."

"No . . ."

"How about you, Charles? Anything on the horizon?"

He grunted a little laugh. "Stan Fogden thinks there might be some more decorating coming up. Let's hope we manage next time without finding a body."

"But no acting work?"

"No. No. 'Fraid not. The 'rest' continues."

"Sorry, Charles. Bad time. There doesn't seem to be a lot around at the moment."

"No, Maurice." Charles looked at the receiver with resignation. "And how was your holiday? How were the Canaries?"

"Well . . ." Maurice's voice made the word long with reservations. "I suppose it was all right. The trouble is, when you've just got a fortnight, you spend the first week untwitching and by the time you start to feel relaxed, you've got to start thinking about coming back again."

"Must be hell," Charles murmured.

"By the way, did you get to see Dana Wilson?"

"Yes."

"Oh, good. Glad I was able to set that up for you, Charles."

"But she's not casting anything in the foreseeable future."

"Oh no, I know *that*. But don't ever say I don't try for you, Charles."

"No. Goodbye, Maurice."

He rang Henry to explain the reasons for his sudden call about the cottage and to fill her in on the details of the case. She listened dutifully, but did not seem very interested. Her mind was elsewhere, and when he had finished the recitation of Bertram Pride's misdoings, the reason became apparent.

"Actually, I'm going back to Gloucestershire next week."

"What, you're giving up the theatre?"

"Well, for a year or two, yes."

"What's suddenly prompted this?"

"Well, you see . . ." She giggled. Charles could imagine the blush spreading over her perfect skin. "James p'd the old q."

"I beg your pardon?"

"Popped the question. Proposed."

"Oh. Er. Congratulations."

"Thanks. Needless to say, I'm chuffed to bits. But we want to get married before Christmas because James has got a tour of duty out in the Falklands coming up, so me and the aged p.s are going to be absolutely flat out with preparations and what-have-you."

"Yes."

"Anyway, sweet of you to ring. V.g. to hear you. We must invite you to the wedding."

But somehow he knew they wouldn't. And, if they had, he somehow didn't think it'd be his scene.

So much for Henry's theatrical career. Her background had reclaimed her. She would lose her virginity to her husband on her wedding night and devote the rest of her life to bringing up squat, doughty little facsimiles of James. She would be happy, she would relate to her children how nearly she became an actress. And her father and sister would say, "I told you so."

Somehow it seemed right.

That evening Charles had an unexpected call.

"It's Frances. Your wife. Remember?"

"It comes back. How are you?"

"Bad."

"David?"

"Yes."

"What?"

"Well, you know we were talking of getting married?"

"Mm."

"And he was going to tell his wife about us while they were on holiday and ask for a divorce?"

"Yes."

"Well, he didn't. And so far as I can tell, he never will. He wants us both. And I think, if he were ever forced into the position of having to make a decision, I'd be the one who went."

"Men are pigs," said Charles automatically. "So what's your relationship now?"

"I don't know." Her voice was tight with emotion. "Charles, can I see you?"

"Yes."

It was a month after the murders at Tryst. Charles Paris had a slight headache as he walked through the underpass beneath the Westway. The previous night he had made yet another valedictory visit to the Montrose.

He was on his way to the Unemployment Office in Lisson Grove to collect his Giro once again.

He needed some cash. He was taking his wife out to dinner that evening.

He met a couple of fellow actors in the queue. A very convivial session in the pub ensued, and Charles's headache dissolved.

None of the other actors had heard of any jobs coming up. The 'rest' looked set fair to continue for ever.

It was after four when he got back to Hereford Road. There was a message for him by the payphone on the landing.

For once the female Swede who had taken it had produced a piece of writing without misleading errors. The message was quite clear.

CHARLES PARIS—PLEASE RING RACHEL GRANT, CASTING DIRECTOR AT THE NATIONAL THEATRE.

175

His hands were sweaty as he fumbled in the directory for the number. His fingers slipped and he had to redial.

But he got through. He asked the voice on the switchboard for Rachel Grant.

"Hello. Rachel Grant."

"Ah, this is Charles Paris. I had a message to call you."

"Yes, yes, of course. Thank you very much for getting back to me so quickly."

There was a silence. "No problem," said Charles fatuously, filling the space.

"The fact is, you were recommended to me, Mr Paris . . ."

"Yes?"

"For a job I need doing . . ."

"Yes?"

"It's the sitting-room of my flat. Just emulsion on the walls and gloss on the paintwork. I wonder, would you be free to do it?"

"Yes," said Charles Paris. "I'd be free."